REMEMBER ME

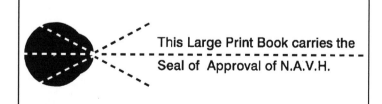

This Large Print Book carries the
Seal of Approval of N.A.V.H.

REGENCY BRIDES, BOOK 3

REMEMBER ME

LOVE CROSSES ENGLAND'S SOCIAL BARRIERS IN THIS HISTORICAL NOVEL

KIMBERLEY COMEAUX

THORNDIKE PRESS

A part of Gale, Cengage Learning

GALE
CENGAGE Learning

Detroit • New York • San Francisco • New Haven, Conn • Waterville, Maine • London

GALE
CENGAGE Learning

Copyright © 2005 by Kimberley Comeaux.
All scripture quotations are taken from the King James Version of the Bible.
Thorndike Press, a part of Gale, Cengage Learning.

LIBRARY OF CONGRESS CATALOGING-IN-PUBLICATION DATA

Comeaux, Kimberley.
  Remember me : love crosses England's social barriers in this historical novel / by Kimberley Comeaux.
    p. cm. — (Regency brides ; bk. 3) (Thorndike Press large print Christian historical fiction)
  ISBN-13: 978-1-4104-1530-1 (hardcover : alk. paper)
  ISBN-10: 1-4104-1530-9 (hardcover : alk. paper)
  1. Large type books. I. Title.
  PS3603.O4728R46 2009
  813'.6—dc22
                                                    2009010881

Published in 2009 by arrangement with Barbour Publishing, Inc.

Printed in the United States of America
1 2 3 4 5 6 7 13 12 11 10 09

Dear Reader,

Ever since I read Jane Austen's *Pride and Prejudice* in the eighth grade, I've been intrigued by the English Regency era. All their rules of conduct and courtly manners were so foreign, yet fascinating to a modern American girl. Through the years I've read and re-read anything I could find on this era, watched every BBC & Masterpiece Theatre movie I could find, and even traveled to England to see the beautiful castles and historical ruins for myself.

So after I finished up a western series I'd written for Heartsong Presents, I decided to write my own Regency romance stories and show how God worked through six people, amidst a society that would often disguise immorality with false modesty and courteous protocol.

The first two stories take place England, but for the third story, I couldn't resist bringing them to my home state of Louisiana. During this period, wars were fought and glorious plantations were built amidst the wild swamps where Indians and alligators reigned. Though our hero and heroine experience quite a culture shock, they still somehow manage to find love!

I hope you enjoy reading about Christina and Nicholas, Catherine and Cameron, and finally Helen and North, as much as I had creating them and even vicariously living through them. Maybe something that they experienced in their Christian journey will encourage or inspire you in your own.

God Bless,
Kimberley Comeaux

To Josie Delonie Kennedy, my grandmother.
And special thanks to Julie Rice and Melissa Alphonso for coming to my rescue
and helping me with this project.

CHAPTER 1

1815

Trevor "North" Kent, the Duke of Northingshire, breathed in the fresh sea air as he
relaxed against the smooth railing of the
ship that was carrying him to America. His
blond, wavy hair, which he'd allowed to
grow longer during the voyage, was blowing
about his face, tickling his nose as he
focused on enjoying his last day aboard ship.
They would be pulling into port in the
morning; and although the voyage had been
a long one, it had been one of much-needed
peace and relaxation, something North
hadn't even realized he required until he
was away from England.

For four years, he'd been planning to
make the trip, where he was to join his
cousins on the sugar plantation that he'd
invested in with them. But because of the
war with England, travel had been made
impossible. Then there had been a personal

matter that had caused him to want to reschedule his trip, also, but it had since been settled to his satisfaction.

The delay had also let him go to the aid of his two best friends: Nicholas, the Earl of Kenswick, and his brother, Lord Thomas Thornton.

The two brothers had been through war, the death of their father, Thomas's shipwreck, and, through all that, raising Thomas's motherless son. North had been there for both of them, giving them advice or just being a friend when they needed it. But now both of them were happily married to two wonderful women, and North was glad to leave the men in their capable hands.

All North wanted was to spend time on the plantation and be free from anyone's problems, except maybe his own. His two cousins were married and hopefully didn't need his advice or support with anything dealing with the state of one's mind or happiness.

Now his own happiness was another kettle of fish altogether, and North had high hopes that he, too, would be able to find love and happiness in his future.

But at the moment, his only concern was how he was to travel and find the plantation, which was located some forty-five miles southwest of New Orleans. He'd sent a message to his cousins telling them of his impending arrival, but the captain had told him that because of the war, mail was slow. It had to be routed through ships going to other countries since there was no travel directly from England. His own journey had been made longer when he'd had to travel to France to board one of their ships.

"The captain has just informed me a storm is headed our way." A Scottish-accented voice spoke beside him, stirring North from his thoughts.

North turned to Hamish Campbell, the minister who was traveling to Louisiana to be the new pastor of a church there. They'd become friends during the long voyage, and North wondered at the troubled look in the older man's eyes. "Well, it is too early in the season to be a hurricane, so I would imagine that it'll pass over us quickly. We are very close to the port, so I don't think there is cause for too much worry," North tried to assure him.

Hamish gripped the railing in front of him as though it were a lifeline. "I know you might think me daft for saying this, but I'm not sure I'll make it to Louisiana."

North stifled a sigh as he felt the need to comfort yet another friend. He knew God

11

was the compelling force in his life who urged him to reach out to people, but he sent up a quick prayer that the Almighty would see fit to give him a little break during his stay in Louisiana.

"Hamish, my dear fellow, these ships are built to withstand storms. Are you sure you are not just experiencing a case of nerves about your new post?"

"Not at all," Hamish insisted, as he reached into his plain, brown coat and pulled out a small, worn Bible. He held it against the rail in both hands, his thumbs stroking the leather cover reverently. "It's . . . it's more of a feeling, I suppose. I've been sensing for some time that my time on earth is almost at an end."

Hamish's words put a chill in North's heart as he struggled to understand. "You are not so old that you will soon die," North reasoned. "And, too, why would God send you all the way over here if He did not mean for you to become the pastor of the church at Golden Bay?"

Hamish didn't answer for a moment. The slightly balding man, who was near North's size and height, just stared off into the now choppy sea as if contemplating his next words. Finally he muttered something that North couldn't decipher and turned to him, his eyes serious. "I think it has something to do with you."

North raised a dark blond brow. "I beg your pardon?"

Hamish nodded his head. "Yes, that must be it! I have felt compelled to befriend you ever since I boarded the ship." He held up his Bible in a strange moment of contemplation and then thrust it toward North, hitting him in the chest. "Take it, please!"

North's hand automatically caught the Bible, but he immediately tried to give it back to Hamish. "What do you mean, 'Take it'? Will you not need this to construct your sermons and what have you?"

Hamish ignored North's attempt to return the small book and turned back toward the railing. "I will not be needing it, I fear. I beg you to take it and —"

Hamish's plea was interrupted when one of the ship's crew ran over to them and gave a brief nod to North. "Your Grace! The captain's askin' all to clear the deck." He pointed out to the increasingly rough waters. "We're lookin' at some bad weather ahead. You could be washed overboard."

North agreed with the young sailor, but when he motioned for Hamish to begin walking toward their cabins, his friend shook his head and pointed to one of the chairs a few feet away from them. "I must retrieve my spectacles. I left them lying on the chair," he insisted as he began to head toward the chair and away from shelter.

The wind was picking up, and North could hear large waves hitting against the ship's hull. It seemed as though the noonday sky had gone from sunny to almost dark in just a matter of minutes. North knew he could not leave Hamish alone, so he tucked the Bible inside his coat and began to walk quickly to him, although the swaying of the ship was making the task very difficult. The ship jolted sharply, and Hamish stumbled and then fell. North was able to grab hold of a deck chair and steady himself before moving to where his friend had fallen.

"Are you all right?" he called loudly over the wind.

Hamish nodded as North helped him stand back up. "I didn't realize the weather could change so fast," he commented as they again steadied themselves against the swaying deck.

North focused on getting them to the chair to retrieve the small, wire-framed spectacles. Once they were finally in Hamish's possession, North led him to the railing. "Use the railing to steady yourself and follow me," he yelled as he looked back to make sure the older man was holding on. Together they began the trek back to their cabin.

A large wave slapped hard against the ship, spraying them both with water. North found it hard to hold on with the chilling wetness making both the railing and the deck slippery. Finally they were mere steps away from the door that led to their cabins. North glanced back to see how Hamish was faring, but his attention was caught by the vast wave that was several feet above the ship and heading straight toward them.

He tried to yell for Hamish to hold on, but there was no time. The water hit both men with more force than either could withstand. As the water swept over the ship, North could feel his body being picked up. Panicked, he tried to keep his head above the water while at the same time looking for his friend. But then pain exploded in the back of North's head. Though he tried to fight unconsciousness, the pain was too great.

His last thought was a prayer that Hamish had somehow managed to keep from being washed overboard.

Two Weeks Later in Golden Bay, Louisiana
The large and rather bored-looking alligator

barely glanced in Helen's direction, despite her yelling and waving a broom about like a madwoman to shoo him away from the house. After about five minutes of this, Helen finally gave up. She plopped herself down on the grass, not even giving a care to her dress as she would have months ago, and glared at the huge reptilian beast.

Before coming to America three months earlier, Helen Nichols had not even heard of an alligator, much less thought that she might stand so close to one.

No, Helen, a gentleman farmer's daughter, had been brought up in her native England with no more cares than what pretty ribbon she'd wear for the day. It had sounded like such a grand adventure when Claudia Baumgartner, granddaughter and heir to the Marquis of Moreland, approached her with the offer of paid companion to her little sister, Josie, in America. Claudia had explained her parents wanted an English girl to provide not only companionship to the lonely girl who lived on her parents' plantation, but also to instruct her in the proper ways of a lady.

But adventure was not the only thing that compelled Helen to leave her family and friends behind. It was the same reason she ventured often to her best friend Christina's home when she heard a certain person had arrived. It was the reason she allowed Christina, who was also the Countess of Kenswick, to provide her a whole new wardrobe for the London season, even though she was mostly snubbed by those who were of much higher class. It was the first thing she thought of in the morning and what she dreamed of at night.

Helen Nichols was in love with North, the Duke of Northingshire.

And the duke was traveling to America, just twenty or so miles from where she was living in Golden Bay.

Helen knew it was foolish to believe that she would even see North while he was staying at his plantation. Yet she knew the Baumgartners, her employers, were acquainted with North's relatives and held out a small hope they would at some point socialize with one another.

She didn't even know if North had arrived in Louisiana. So day after day, she'd keep a keen ear out to hear any news about the Kent plantation. So far, though, she'd heard nothing.

"What are you doing?" A young voice sounded behind her. Josie Baumgartner, Helen's precocious thirteen-year-old charge, skipped around and plopped down in front of her. With wildly curly brown hair, freck-les, and a mischievous gleam constantly glowing in her hazel eyes, Josie looked just like the wild child that she was. In fact, Helen despaired of ever turning the young girl into anything remotely resembling a proper lady. She liked to ride astride horses, fish while wading in the swamp, and climb trees. Those were the seminormal things she did. The other activities consisted of playing practical jokes, collecting every creepy-crawly thing she could find, and voicing her opinion about every subject her father and mother would bring up at the dinner table, usually expressing an opposing view.

But despite her incorrigible behavior that would likely leave most of English society agog, she was an extremely likable girl with a personality that made it hard to reprimand her or be angry with her for long.

Helen sighed as she answered Josie's ques-tion. "I am trying to get this big lizard to move away from the front door so I can go into the house." She pointed at the ugly beast. "But it seems he is determined to ignore my commands."

Josie giggled. "We have five other doors, you know. Why don't you just go through one of those?" she reasoned in her drawn-out American accent.

Helen sniffed. "It's the principle of the thing, my dear. I will not be ruled by a slimy green creature!"

Josie jumped up and crept closer to the alligator, though still at a safe distance. "Did you know they eat small animals? Dorie Le-Beau said one ate her cat once."

Helen shivered with disgust. "Well, that's just uncivilized, isn't it?"

Josie turned back to Helen with a look of long-suffering. "You think *everything* is uncivilized if it's not from England."

Helen stood and brushed off the skirt of her gown. "Well, of course I do," she stated matter-of-factly. "We're the most civilized people in the world!" She had a brief recollection of Christina and herself running about the countryside with dirty dresses and faces. They were forever rolling about with puppies and kittens and trespassing on others' property to climb their trees. Not a very civilized way to behave for a couple of young ladies.

Helen wisely kept the memory to herself.

"Well, we can go get Sam to come over here and kill it. They make for pretty good eating, you know," Josie said, interrupting Helen's thoughts. Sam Youngblood was a Choctaw Indian who lived on property adjoining the plantation. He also fancied

19

himself in love with Helen and was forever trying to barter horses or cows with Mr. Baumgartner for her. He said it was the Choctaw way.

Helen told him the practice of bartering for a woman was just plain barbaric!

Helen shivered again as she got back to Josie's comment. *"Ladies* do not *eat —"*

"I know, I know," Josie interjected. "Ladies do not eat *anything* that *crawls* around on its belly. It's *quite* uncivilized!" she mocked, using Helen's higher-pitched English accent.

"Scoff if you must, but you will do well to —"

"Miss Helen! Miss Josie!" a male voice called out from behind them. They turned to see George, the Baumgartners' house servant who usually ran their errands in town, running up the dusty drive.

Though the Baumgartners owned many slaves to run the vast plantation that consisted of thousands of acres, a sugar mill, the slave and servant quarters, not to mention the huge three-story white mansion, they had freed many of those who worked in the house and the higher-ranking field hands. The Baumgartners were good people who treated every worker and slave fairly, but Helen secretly felt the whole slave system was unjust and inhumane.

"What is it, George?" Josie asked as he stopped before them and tried to catch his breath.

"The preacher . . ." His voice cracked as he took another deep breath. "They found him. He ain't dead like they thought."

Helen and Josie exchanged a disbelieving look. "You mean he did not drown as we were all told?" Helen attempted to comprehend. Just over a week ago, the people of Golden Bay had been informed that the preacher for whom they'd been waiting had fallen overboard with another man and had drowned. The Baumgartners, LeBeau, and Whitakers were all distressed and saddened, since it was these neighboring families who had gotten together to build a church and then pay for his voyage from Scotland.

If this news was true, they wouldn't have to go to the trouble of searching for another minister!

"A couple of fishermen pulled 'im out of the gulf and took 'im back to they cabins 'bout thirty or so miles from here," George explained. "They sez that he didn't wake up fer about fo' days, but they found a Bible on him that had his name on it. They sez he didn't know who he was when he finally woke up, but after they told 'im his name

21

and that he was a preacher headed for our town, he seemed to remember."

Josie clasped her hands together. "Why, that sounds like a bona fide miracle!" she exclaimed. "Is he in town? Can we go see him?"

"Yes'm, Miss Josie, you sho' can. That's why I ran back lickety-split." He ran the back of his sleeve across his beaded brow. "They's wantin' the mastah to come out and give 'im a proper welcome with any food or house gifts to help 'im get settled."

"Oh, this is exciting, isn't it?" Helen whispered eagerly as she looked from George to Josie. "It will be so refreshing going to a proper service again instead of waiting for the circuit preacher to pass by. It will be just like it was in —"

"England! We know; we know," Josie finished for her with exasperation. "Let's just hurry up and tell my parents so we can meet him!"

It didn't take long for the family to assemble the goods they had set aside for the new preacher and to load their wagon and carriage. Ten or so minutes later, they pulled into the small town that consisted of the blacksmith, a general store, and the newly built church. The town was actually owned by three plantations, unlike many others along the river that were self-contained. The three families signed an agreement that they would share the profits from the businesses, as well as the labor to keep them running.

There was already a small crowd in the tiny yard of the church, with its small parsonage on the side. Mr. and Mrs. Baumgartner stepped out of the carriage first, followed by Josie and Helen.

As they drew nearer, Josie walked on her tiptoes, trying to see over everyone's heads. Helen, herself, tried to see around them but could only see the top of a man's head. In fact, the hair was such a pretty golden blond, a person couldn't help but notice through all the dark heads gathered around him.

Helen was finally close enough to see better, and as the crowd parted, she was disappointed to see the man's back was turned as he spoke with Mr. Baumgartner. She studied his longish, wavy hair, then the width of his broad shoulders for a moment. He seemed almost familiar to Helen, as if she had met the gentleman before, yet she was sure she had never heard of a Hamish Campbell until she had arrived in Louisiana.

"Oh, I wish Papa would turn him around so we could see him! I had imagined he would be an older man, but he appears to be younger than I thought," Josie whispered as their neighbors chatted excitedly around them.

"Indeed," Helen murmured, as she tried to inch her way closer to him. She noticed he was quite tall. Though they seemed to be a little ragged and faded, his clothes were very well made, cut like those worn by the nobility.

When she finally was able to hear him speak, Helen suddenly realized who the preacher reminded her of.

He was the same height and build and sounded just like . . . North, the Duke of Northingshire.

Helen briefly rubbed her brow, thinking that of course she must be mistaken and perhaps had been in the sun too long. The preacher was supposed to be a Scotsman, and the accent she thought she heard was clearly a cultured English one.

"Ah! Here are my wife and daughter," Mr. Baumgartner said, motioning toward Helen's direction. "Let me introduce you."

As she began to turn, Josie bumped her as she scrambled to go to her father, and then Mrs. Baumgartner stepped in front of her, again blocking her view. She heard the man speak to her employer and his daughter and again was struck by his rich voice.

I just miss North. I am clearly hallucina—

"And this is Josie's companion, Miss Helen Nichols, who has come from England and been with us for three months now," she heard Mrs. Baumgartner say, as she stepped back. For the first time, Helen got a view of the tall man's face.

For a moment Helen said nothing, frozen by the sheer shock of seeing the man before her.

It *was* North!

And he was smiling pleasantly at her without so much as a gleam of recognition shining in his light blue gaze.

"Pleased to make your acquaintance, Miss Nichols," he responded smoothly with a nod.

Helen was horrified that he did not recognize her. She had spent many hours in his presence in the past and thought it humiliating that she didn't seem familiar to him at all. But then she had a second thought: *Why is he pretending to be a preacher?*

Confused, she found herself blurting, "North? Do you not remember me?"

CHAPTER 2

An immediate hush fell over the group as every eye turned to stare at Helen, including North. Helen focused only on him as she watched the strange expressions move across his handsome, strong face.

At first it appeared to be fear, then it went to what looked like confusion, and then it was as though a mask fell across his face, shielding her from his thoughts entirely. He seemed to compose himself as he nervously glanced around the group and then turned his gaze back to Helen.

His eyes were unreadable as he smiled at her and finally responded. "Of course I do. It's just . . . I suppose it has been quite awhile, hasn't it?" Helen wasn't sure if he was telling or asking. Neither would make a bit of sense to Helen since she'd only seen him four months ago. "It is good to have a friend nearby," he finished cryptically, perplexing her even more.

She was about to ask him what he was doing here, but he turned from her suddenly, stopping any further communication between them.

Doubts assailed her as she thought maybe the man wasn't North after all. Perhaps he had a cousin who looked like him.

But then, she amended her thoughts, why did he pretend to know her?

Oh, it was very vexing on her nerves to reason his behavior all out in her mind.

"You know him?" Josie exclaimed, startling Helen back to the present. "Why didn't you tell us you knew the preacher?"

Helen shook her head absently as her eyes stayed on who she was sure was the Duke of Northingshire. "I didn't know his Christian name. I've always called him North," she lied, since she knew very well that his name was Trevor Kent and certainly *not* Hamish Campbell!

Josie frowned. "You addressed a preacher by calling him North? That's strange and not at all the civilized thing for a lady to do." She paused for effect. "According to you."

Helen licked her lips nervously as she tried to answer without too much lying involved. "I knew him when he wasn't a minister." She finally dragged her eyes away from the confusing man and tried to appear nonchalant. "I don't suppose I knew him as well as I thought." That was an understatement!

"Well, you shall have plenty of time to get to know him in the future," Josie reasoned, as she took Helen's hand and pulled her toward the nice lawn beside the church. "Let's sit over there and wait for my parents."

Helen agreed and allowed Josie to pull her to the white wooden benches, which were placed under a great oak shade tree.

As soon as they sat down, Josie immediately brought their conversation back to the preacher. "Don't you think he is the most handsome man you've ever seen? And to think you know him!" she expressed in a lovelorn tone. She sat up and looked at Helen as if she were suddenly hit with an idea. "He is unmarried, and you are unmarried! You would make a great match!"

If only it could be so, Helen thought longingly. But until she figured out why North was pretending to be someone else, she could not even wish for it. "Josie, he did not even recognize me. How could you think he would want to marry a lady who has made no lasting impression in his mind?" She sighed. "Besides, I am here to work and teach you to be a lady. Wishing that I would fall in love with North just so you will not have to learn your lessons on etiquette will only bring you a headache."

Josie sat back on the bench and groaned. "Why does being a lady seem so *boring?*"

Helen hid a grin. "One day when you become interested in a young man, he'll expect you to act like a lady, and then you will thank God I bored you so!"

"I will never be interested in boys!" she declared.

"That is too bad, for I have a feeling you will grow up to be quite a lovely woman one day." A man's voice spoke beside them.

Startled, Helen turned and looked up to find North standing over her. "North!" she exclaimed automatically but then quickly amended, "I'm sorry. I mean *Reverend.*"

He seemed preoccupied as he presented her a small smile. North quickly stepped closer, whispering in an urgent voice, "I must speak to you alone, Miss Nichols." He nervously glanced around as if to see if anyone was watching him and then looked briefly at Josie. "There is some very important information I need, and I'm positive that only you can help me."

Helen felt butterflies of excitement fluttering about in her chest, just as she always did when North spoke to her. It didn't matter if he was acting like the craziest man alive or that he was pretending to be a minister, which Helen imagined was a big faux pas in God's book! All that mattered was North, the love of her life, had asked to talk to her. Alone!

She jumped up with more enthusiasm than was warranted, for she startled both Josie and North. "Of course, you can speak with me!" she said brightly as she reached down to pull Josie up from the bench. "Please be a dear and excuse us, will you, Josie?" She threw the request to her charge without so much as a glance and then latched her arm around North's elbow. "Let's walk, shall we?"

North looked a little dazed but gave her a tentative smile. "Not too far. I would not want to bring suspicion on your character or mine. I may not remember much, but I do know that talking alone with a young woman out in the open public is considered a social blunder if she is not accompanied by a chaperone."

Helen stopped suddenly upon hearing his words, let go of his arm, and turned to stand in front of him. "Did you just say that you might not remember much?" She shook her head. "What does that mean?"

North stood there, staring down at her,

looking more handsome than ever before. His countenance, however, was not the easygoing and self-assured gentleman she'd known in England. Instead he looked tired, confused, and not at all the confident man he should be.

He took a deep breath as he stared off to his left for a moment, then slowly brought his gaze back to her. "I do not remember who I am." Helen gasped, but North held out his hand so that he might continue. "I apparently fell off the ship that I had been on during a storm. Two fishermen dragged me out of the water and brought me to shore, where I finally came to my senses. But that is where every one of my memories begins. I wouldn't even know my name except I had a Bible inside my coat that had the name Hamish Campbell etched into the leather."

Helen could not even speak for being so dumbfounded by his story. She had never heard of a person forgetting his own name and past. "So you don't remember anything? Not your family, friends, or any sort of past memory?"

He shook his head as he walked past her to lean against the oak.

"And no one knows you've lost your

memory?" she asked as she walked over to him.

"No, I didn't want to make everyone think I'd lost my mind or had become crazed." He took a minute to rub the back of his head, then continued. "To tell you the truth, when the fisherman who I was staying with finally told me he'd found out where I was heading and that I was to be the vicar of a church in Louisiana, I felt even more confused. I pretended, however, that I suddenly remembered." He looked back to Helen. "That is why I am so anxious to talk to you. You know who I am. You and you alone can tell me about myself, what kind of family background I have or anything that might possibly help me to remember . . . *something!*" His eyes bore into hers as if he were trying to read her thoughts. "You can also confirm I am indeed who they say I am or if it is some sort of mistake." He paused and seemed to try calming himself with a deep breath. "Helen, am I the Reverend Hamish Campbell?"

Helen opened her mouth to inform him that he definitely was *not* the good reverend but stopped before any words could escape. A thought suddenly seized her — a truly wicked thought.

If North knew he was a duke — a nobleman — sixth in line to the throne of England, then Helen could never hope to win his affections, for he would be socially far above her station.

But as a reverend . . .

Oh, surely she could not consider it, much less go through with such a deed! But she could not help it. If North believed he was a reverend, then he would be in the same class as she. The barrier of position and means would no longer be an obstacle, and the brotherly affection North always showed toward her could change into something more if he believed he was Hamish Campbell.

"Miss Nichols? Were you indeed telling the truth when you said you knew me? You suddenly seem confused about . . ."

"You are!" she blurted out before she could think twice about it. "I . . . I mean . . . you are . . . the reverend . . . Hamish Campbell," she stammered, as she began to already feel the weight of the lie she had just told.

He let out a breath as he ran a hand through his shimmering blond curls. "I was hoping . . ." He paused and began again. "I don't know what I was hoping. It's just that I do not feel like a Hamish Campbell. I cannot imagine choosing to be a vicar, either. I do have a sense I am a follower of God and have attended church in my past, but . . . being a vicar does not seem to . . . *fit!*" He threw his hand in the air with frustration.

If he only knew! Helen thought guiltily. "What sort of man did you imagine yourself to be?"

North seemed to think a minute before he answered. "I really don't know, except I look at my clothes and, though they are faded and worn from being wet and then dried in the sun, I somehow know they are very finely made and that the fabrics are not something a poor man would wear." He held up his long, lean hands. "I look at my palms and see no evidence of calluses from hard work."

"Perhaps you spent your time in studying and contemplation," Helen inserted.

"I suppose you could be right, but it doesn't explain the clothes."

All the lies were making Helen very nervous, and she wasn't finished telling them yet. "Perhaps your family is somewhat wealthy, but as you were the youngest son, you chose the church as your occupation," she improvised.

He raised a dark blond brow. "Perhaps? You mean you don't know?"

"Uh . . ." Helen scrambled to answer him

34

without telling another lie. "We were introduced through a mutual acquaintance and saw each other only a few times after that," she answered truthfully.

His expression fell to a frown. "Then you don't know me well enough to tell me anything significant?"

Helen breathed a sigh of relief, hoping that this revelation would stop his questions. "I am sorry, but no." She looked toward the crowd and noticed the Baumgartners were looking her way. "I'd better go. My employers are about to leave."

She started to walk off, but he stopped her by touching her arm. "Wait! May I ask you one more question?"

Seeing the confusion in his beautiful blue eyes, Helen could not turn down his request. "Of course you may."

"Everyone keeps telling me I have journeyed here from Scotland, yet I clearly do not have a Scottish accent. Do you know anything about this?"

This question she could answer truthfully. "Actually, I do. You were raised in England, but later when your family bought an estate in Scotland, you would spend summers there. I suppose you've moved back there recently." She felt compelled to put her hand over his. "Good-bye, Nor . . . er . . . I mean, Reverend. I'm sorry I was not more helpful."

He gave her a small, preoccupied smile, nodded, then stepped away from her.

Helen took one last look back before she ran to where her employers were waiting for her. As she suspected, they were full of questions.

"You must tell us how you know our new preacher, Helen!" Mrs. Baumgartner ordered immediately as they settled in the carriage. Imogene Baumgartner looked much younger than her forty years. Though she didn't have the style the ladies in England had in the way of clothes or hairstyles, she was always very prettily dressed in her flowered cotton and linen gowns that she so preferred, her dark brown hair knotted low on her neck.

Robert Baumgartner, on the other hand, sat quietly, as he usually did whenever his wife was going on about something, preferring the solitude of his thoughts as he looked out of the carriage window. Helen often wondered if he regretted his choice of marrying the daughter of his father's butler. After all, it caused him to be disinherited by his father and, in turn, to renounce his claim to the title of Marquis of Moreland. Josie had told Helen they'd taken his small inheritance from his mother and moved to America soon after.

It seemed like such a grand love story, and since Helen was also in love with a man above her station, it gave her a small hope her own life could have a happy ending with North by her side.

"Helen, dear?" Mrs. Baumgartner prompted, shaking Helen from her thoughts.

After remembering her employer had asked how she knew North, Helen answered, "I knew him briefly through a friend." She wished Mrs. Baumgartner would take the hint that she did not want to talk about it, but the woman was very persistent when she wanted to know something.

Imogene stared at her as if waiting for more, but when Helen remained silent, she tried again. "He certainly was wearing a very fine suit of clothes to be a poor vicar. I almost had the feeling when studying his bearing and regal pose that he might be a nobleman!" She leaned closer to Helen from across the carriage. "Do you know if he is indeed from a noble family?"

Helen could feel sweat beading on her forehead, and it wasn't just because of the humidity. "I know he is from a wealthy family."

That answer seemed to be enough for Imogene. She leaned back and folded her arms as if pleased with herself. "Of course he is. I am quite good at spotting a gentleman of means." She paused and frowned. "Although he must be quite a younger son and not entitled to the wealth if he has chosen to be a clergyman."

"Must he?" Helen answered, trying desperately not to lie.

"Well, of course he must!" Imogene declared. "But his misfortune is our good luck. I had not looked forward to trying to find another vicar to take his place."

The questions seemed to be at an end as they rode the rest of the way in silence. But Helen's reprieve was only a brief one.

"Helen, it just occurred to me he might be a good match for you!" Imogene exclaimed as they exited the carriage.

Josie piped up. "I had told her the same thing!"

Imogene clasped her hands together as if thrilled with her idea. "You are a gentleman's daughter, Helen, and he is a gentleman! If you married him, you could stay right here in Golden Bay with us. Wouldn't that be just the thing?"

Just thinking about living in the rugged, swampy lands of Louisiana forever made Helen shiver with horror. But on the other hand, if she could spend her life with North by her side . . . perhaps it might not be so bad.

"I barely know him . . . ," she prevaricated, but Imogene was not one to let anything distract her.

"We have all the time in the world for that!" she declared as the carriage slowed to a stop in front of the home. "Leave it to me, dear, and you shall see yourself wed by fall!"

As Helen climbed out of the carriage behind Imogene and Josie, she wished her employer's words could be true, but if North remembered who he was before he could fall in love with her, her hopes of even being his friend would be permanently dashed.

CHAPTER 3

The more North learned of his life, the more confused he became. Many days and long hours since he was rescued, he tried to find just the tiniest of memories, just the smallest tidbit to help him feel less lost, less bewildered.

The only information he'd heard that felt as though it belonged to him was when Helen Nichols had called him North. The more he said it to himself, the more the name seemed to fit him, as though he'd finally had one little piece of his missing life back.

But saying it did not bring back any more memories or any other sense of familiarity like he hoped and prayed it would. There was nothing in his mind other than a few memories since he'd awakened. The rest was this large, gaping black hole that refused to give up any answers.

Now as he sat in the tiny house the church

leaders had shown him to, with its two rooms divided only by a large piece of cloth, he felt more out of his element than ever.

Since he had nothing but his deep-down gut feeling to rely on, North assumed he had never lived in such a small, barren house, nor had he ever known anyone who had. Before they had left him, he'd been shown the barn behind the house, where a cow and a few chickens were kept. He trusted the feeling of dismay that washed over him when they told him the animals would give him all the milk, eggs, and poultry he could eat.

They actually expected him to *milk* the cow and somehow get eggs out from *under* the chickens. Then, if he actually wanted to *eat* chicken, he would have to *kill* one to have it?

Appalling!

He almost told them so, but when they said that North should be familiar with the animals since he had been raised on a farm, North bit back any retort he had been about to make.

Helen Nichols had left out that little piece of news. If his family had been wealthy, why would he be milking his own cows?

Confusion crowded his mind as he thought about it. Perhaps they'd lost their money, he tried to reason, which is why he never tried to pursue a deeper acquaintance with Helen Nichols.

Oh, yes, those thoughts had run through his mind when she'd informed him they barely knew one another. The very first thing that popped into his head was he must have been a blind fool to let such a beautiful, delightful woman slip in and out of his life so easily.

And she *was* beautiful, with her inky black curls that fell about her rosy cheeks and those dark blue eyes that seemed to look right though him, straight to his heart.

When he realized he was contemplating pursuing a woman instead of focusing on his immediate problem, he jumped up from his hard, wooden seat and stomped out of the cottage.

As he breathed in the cooling air that the darkening sky had blown in from the gulf, North strove to find some sort of peace, anything to take away the uncertainty plaguing his heart and mind. Spying the church that was in front of his cottage, he began to walk toward it. The church leaders had told him the building had been used seldom, only when a traveling preacher was in the area.

North thought it looked as lonely as he

was, standing there empty with its freshly painted walls and its dark, gleaming windowpanes. Again North tried to look inside himself, to find some sort of connection with the church, to feel the calling he must have had — but he came up empty.

God must surely have some reason for taking away his memory, North tried to rationalize. Perhaps in his forgotten past he needed to learn a valuable lesson, or perhaps someone's life would benefit from his dilemma. Of course, he couldn't think of one thing that would benefit anyone, but he was only a man; God was all-knowing, so there must be a reason.

Briefly North reached out and braced both hands on the smoothed planks of the church. "Help me, dear Lord, to remember. If I have been called by You to serve as Your minister, then I want to know that certainty once again. I am frightened by what lies ahead of me, Lord, and I have an idea that I don't feel this way normally. But most of all, dear God, please do not let me fail these people." He stopped as he once again felt the enormity of his situation bearing down on him. "In Jesus' name. Amen." He finished quickly and backed away from the church.

He was about to walk back to his cottage

when the sound of horse hooves broke the calm silence of the night.

North immediately recognized the two-wheeled, small curricle as being one of excellent quality, though he wished he understood *how* he knew this! Instead of focusing on the frustration that was boiling up within him, he watched as a tall, slim, brown man climbed down from the conveyance and walked toward him. The man was dressed in a black suit with a fluffy white cravat tied at his neck. North noticed there was an air of self-confidence about him in his walk and posture, and he wondered, not for the first time, about the class system within the slave and nonslave community.

"Reverend Campbell," the man's deep voice sounded as he gave him a brief bow. North returned the gesture, and the man continued. "I've been sent by Mr. and Mrs. Baumgartner, sir, of the Golden Bay plantation. They would like to extend to you an invitation to dine with them this evening."

Food! It was the only thing that stood out in North's nutrition-starved mind. He was invited to eat food he wouldn't have to cook, milk, or kill.

"Oh, this dress is wrong!" Helen wailed as she stood in front of her mirror, critically

44

surveying the light blue taffeta. "The ribbon is wrinkled, and the material just droops in this heat!" She dramatically grabbed two handfuls of hair on either side of her head. "And just look at my hair! It will do nothing but curl! I look like a ragamuffin."

Millie, the young slave woman who served both Helen and Josie, propped her hands on her slim hips and made a *tsk*-ing noise as she shook her head. "Miss Helen, I don't know what's wrong with yo' eyes, honey chil', but there ain't nothin' wrong with that dress or yo' hair." Millie took Helen's arm, pulled her away from the mirror, and directed her to sit at her dressing table. "Now yo' jus' got yo'self all in a lather 'cause o' that young man who's comin' to dinnah, tha's all! Now sit still and let me fix yo' hair up real pretty."

Josie took that particular moment to let herself in the room without so much as a knock. "I knew it! I knew she was sweet on the preacher!" she crowed with delight.

Millie stopped brushing Helen's hair to shake the brush in Josie's direction. "Miss Josie, I done tol' ya and tol' ya. You gonna listen at the wrong do' one day, and it's gonna get yo' in a mess o' trouble!" She pointed the brush to the chair next to Helen. "Now sit yo'self down, and I'll get

45

to yo' hair next."

Josie did as she was told because Millie, slave or no, just had the kind of voice you obeyed. It was then Helen noticed the dress the younger girl was wearing.

"Josie, you can't wear that old dress to dinner!" she blurted with horror.

Josie frowned as she looked down at the plain beige dress made of slightly wrinkled cotton. "What's wrong with it? I've worn this to dinner lots of times, and you've never said anything about it."

Helen took a deep breath to calm her nerves, and then in her best teacher's voice, she instructed, "When guests are dining with your family, you must dress in a more formal manner." She noticed Millie looking for a hairpin and opened her drawer to find one for her. She then continued. "Especially when you have a guest like the d—" She stumbled over the word *duke* and quickly corrected herself. "Er, North."

Josie let out a breath to show her frustration with the whole conversation. "He's just the preacher. It's not like he's the president of the United States."

No. More like the Duke of Northingshire. If Helen's nerves were this frazzled with trying to keep her story straight and not saying the wrong thing, how was it going to be in

46

front of North?

What a mess she'd gotten herself into!

In the end, Josie kept her plain dress on, and with her hair done up "pretty" by Millie, Helen decided, droopy or not, her dress would have to do, also. She noticed as she approached the three adults that the Baumgartners wore their usual casual attire; and when she saw North, she was glad they did.

Of course he would have no other clothes! How silly of her not to remember that all his belongings had not been brought from the ship. And even when they were, would he realize the garments belonged to someone else? Would he remember that his own trunks contained the finest clothes England had to offer and not those of a poor vicar?

She had to remind herself not to get into a mental tizzy as she walked up and greeted him.

"Hello, Reverend," she greeted, as she tried to ignore the guilt she felt over calling him that false title. "Are you getting settled in?"

The smile he gave her was lacking in confidence, and his words were those of someone putting on a brave front . . . and failing at it. "Uh, yes, I think so. I'll just need time to adjust to the . . . uh . . . culture change."

The Baumgartners all laughed at that, and though Helen joined them, it was only out of politeness. Since she, too, was still experiencing quite a culture shock, it was difficult to joke about it just yet.

They were all seated in the dining room, which boasted a long table that could easily seat sixteen people. Helen was not accustomed to such extravagance, since her own family manor was of modest means. Neither was she accustomed to all the house servants who worked around the clock to make sure the family had all they needed.

No, she wasn't accustomed to such a lifestyle, but she knew North was. This was apparent only to her as she watched him walk into the room without so much as blinking at the expensively carved furnishings or the heavy blue brocade-and-satin drapes framing the ten large windows in the room. The only thing that caused him to pause was when he noticed the large cloth-covered fan above the table that was framed in the same carvings as the table and chairs. Attached to the fan was a blue satin cord that ran along the high ceiling all the way to the corner, where a small child was pulling it, causing the fan to swoosh back and forth, creating a breeze.

"Remarkable" was the only comment North made as he seated himself by Mrs. Baumgartner and across from Helen. There was a smattering of small talk as they were served their first course, and Helen noticed North was clever enough to keep the conversation off himself by inquiring about the plantation and Mr. Baumgartner's plans for it. Under normal circumstances, it might have been enough; however, North had never dealt with Imogene Baumgartner.

"Oh, enough about business! You must tell us about yourself, Reverend. I quite expected you to have a Scottish dialect and am curious as to why you do not," she voiced, interrupting the gentlemen's conversation.

Helen could actually see the nervous sweat start to bead on North's brow as he paused before answering. "I was raised in England but spent summers with my family in Scotland. I later moved there, but my accent was already established," he answered, parroting the explanation she'd given him earlier.

"And what town were you from in England?" she persisted.

North glanced briefly her way, and Helen could see the rising panic in his eyes. He had no idea where he was from, and Helen scrambled for a way to answer for him. Her only problem was that by saying the name of Northingshire, it might make him remember suddenly who he was. So she thought of the town next to it.

"Lanchester, isn't it? In County Durham? I believe you mentioned that town when we last saw one another," she blurted out, and from the odd looks by the Baumgartners, she knew her answering for him in such a forceful manner seemed quite odd.

But North adeptly smoothed the awkward moment, as would anyone used to handling all manner of social affairs. "Yes, I used to call Lanchester home. Excellent memory, Miss Nichols," he answered easily. Helen was amazed that, though he couldn't remember his own name, he still acted like the nobleman he actually was.

Helen prayed his answers would satisfy Mrs. Baumgartner, but to no avail. "And your parents, are they still living?" Imogene asked.

Once again, his panicked gaze flew to Helen, and once again, she intervened. "Oh, I meant to tell you how sorry I am that I was not able to attend your father's funeral." Helen looked at Mrs. Baumgartner, who she noticed was looking a little put out by her interruptions, and added, "It was influenza. His mother, however, still lives in Scotland."

North seemed to be digesting what she'd just said, and Helen had to add one more lie she would have to beg forgiveness for later. In truth, she didn't know how his father had died. She only knew he'd become duke at the age of ten.

North's panic was now curiosity as he looked in her direction, and she could tell he was trying to remember what she'd told him.

"Really, Helen!" Mrs. Baumgartner scolded, causing both of them to look to her. "I really think that the Reverend Campbell can answer my questions himself."

"I'm sorry, ma'am," Helen apologized as she forced herself to look contrite. In truth, she was just plain stressed by the position she'd put both North and herself in. But it was too late to fix it now! What was she to do? Quickly she scrambled to find a reasonable, believable explanation for her behavior. "I suppose I am just excited about seeing a familiar face from England."

Helen couldn't have come up with a more perfect excuse. Immediately Imogene's expression changed; she thought she knew a secret as she slid her gaze from North to Helen and back again. "Of course you are, dear!" she crooned as she put a hand to her chest and sighed. "I forgot you haven't had a chance to reacquaint yourselves."

"So do you holler when you preach?" Josie piped up in her usual straightforward fashion.

"Well, my word, Josie! What a thing to ask!" her mother reprimanded her.

The thirteen-year-old shrugged. "Well, the preacher at Joseph's church down the bayou hollers. Joseph says it is because the preacher wants to make sure the devil knows they won't fall for his tricks."

Helen quickly covered her mouth with her napkin to conceal her laughter, and when she looked across the table, she noticed North was having a hard time containing his own.

"Maybe it is because sometimes the preacher believes his *congregation* is hard of hearing when he sees them doing something that isn't right," North suggested when he had his laughter under control.

Josie nodded sagely, unaware she was entertaining them all. "You could be right, Reverend. So *do* you holler, too?"

North appeared to think about it and then answered, "I don't believe I have ever hollered in church."

Helen had to cover her mouth again when

she pictured North "hollering" at all. He was much too dignified. Again, North slid his gaze Helen's way and shared a smile with her.

Their look apparently did not go unnoticed, although it may have been misread. Surprising them all, the usually silent Mr. Baumgartner spoke up. "Why don't you walk him out to the bayou, Helen, and show him our newly built pier? It is a full moon tonight, so there should be plenty of light. It will give you two a chance to get reacquainted." He took a drink of water and then continued. "I'll have Joseph follow you at a distance to act as a chaperone."

Helen stared at her usually quiet employer, and she was further surprised when he gave her a brief wink that only she could see. "All right," she murmured, looking back at North. "Would you like to see the bayou?"

A look of pure relief relaxed North's strong, manly face, and a smile curved his lips. "Only if you tell me what a bayou is."

They all laughed at his comment, and Helen stood up from her chair. "It will be better if I show you."

In a matter of moments, Helen and North

were walking the path that led out to the pier.

"I want to apologize for putting you in the position of having to answer for me," North told her as he looked over at her, admiring how the moon illuminated her soft features. "But I thought you said you didn't know much about me." He hoped she knew more than she let on, not only for the sake of getting his memory back, but because it might mean that she'd been interested enough in him to find out.

She didn't answer right away, and when she did, there was regret on her face as she gave him a quick glance. "I'm afraid I told a small lie in there just now." She blew out a breath and stepped in front of him to stop him from walking. "I lied about your father."

He had trouble focusing on what she was saying, so drawn was he by her beauty and the soft tones of her voice. But when he did realize what she'd said, he frowned in confusion. "What are you saying? That he is alive?"

She seemed horrified by his question as she put her hands on either side of her face. "Oh no! I didn't mean that. . . . I mean . . . he is deceased." She shook her head. "Oh, dear! I meant he didn't die of the flu like I said. I hope I did not give you false hope."

North reached out and took her hands from her face, squeezed them, and let them go. "You didn't injure me, Miss Nichols. When you said my father had died, I instinctively knew you were right. I can't explain how I know this, but it was the same when you called me 'North.' " He thought for a moment. "Do you know my mother?"

Helen looked regretful when she shook her head. "I'm sorry, but no. I never met her, nor do I know anything about her."

He sighed. "It seems a shame not to remember one's own mother." He smiled at her wistfully. "It seems a shame not to remember you, either."

Helen looked up at him for a moment, making North wish even more for his memories back, if only the ones he had of this lovely, enchanting woman who was gazing into his eyes. Then she seemed to grow uncomfortable with the intimacy of their situation. The moment was over when she turned to resume their walk to the pier.

When they arrived at the pier, she announced to him that the stream of water that looked like a small river was the bayou they had spoken of. From there, she explained, smaller ships and barges could move their sugarcane out to the gulf.

They discussed the merits of such a

waterway awhile longer but soon fell silent. Helen and North stood there a moment, letting cool air off the bayou's water flow over them as they breathed in the sweet smell of the magnolia blossoms on the nearby trees.

"Did you know my house has only two rooms?" he commented, finally breaking the silence with an odd subject.

She looked up at him and laughed. "I beg your pardon?"

He held up two fingers to her but kept his gaze looking over the water. "Only two. A bedroom and a living room that has a large fireplace from which I am supposed to cook my meals."

From the corner of his eye, he saw her cover her mouth to hide her smile. "Oh, dear. I didn't realize it was so small," she said in a muffled voice from behind her fingers.

"Can you tell me, Miss Nichols: Have I ever lived in such a small house before?"

"Uh . . . no," she answered with certainty. This time a giggle escaped.

"No, no. Go ahead and laugh. I expect I shall get used to it. At least that is my goal."

She laughed, and he joined in with her. It went a long way in releasing the stress he'd felt ever since arriving at Golden Bay.

"I must have been prepared for such a life of imposed poverty. Why else would I have journeyed to such a primitive part of the United States to be their pastor?" he said after their laughter had subsided.

He watched as apprehension seemed to cloud her eyes for a moment. She looked away quickly but then looked back up at him. "North . . . I mean . . . Reverend . . ."

"Please call me North," he insisted, since it was the only thing that made his life seem real.

"North," she said his name softly. "There is something I need to tell you —"

"Can you tell me something?" he interrupted, barely hearing her words. He knew he had to ask his next question, because it had burned constantly in his heart since the moment he laid eyes on her. "Did I ever call on you or ever do anything to make you think I wanted to see you more?"

"No, but you really must hear what I —"

"You see, that is what I cannot figure out." He continued, as if she hadn't spoken. "Why didn't I call on you? Did you have a beau, or for that matter, *do* you have one?"

She stood there frozen, as if shocked by what he was asking. "I've never had a beau."

Elation swept over North as she spoke those precious words. It suddenly didn't matter why he had not pursued her in the past. There was nothing stopping him now.

"Excellent!" he exclaimed with a wide grin. He held out his arm to her. "Shall we go back to the house?"

She did as he asked, but he could tell she didn't understand his response or his delight. That didn't matter.

It wouldn't be long until she realized he was determined to be her first and *only* beau.

CHAPTER 4

When North awoke the next morning, he was disappointed to find his memory had not improved. He didn't even feel as though he was close to remembering anything. He tried to recall if he'd dreamed of anything, and yet he knew his dreams had only consisted of one thing . . . Helen.

In his dreams, she was smiling and gazing into his eyes; North was fairly sure it wasn't a dream of his past with her, but a dream of what he wished would happen.

Slowly North pulled himself from his bed and once again found himself shocked by the bareness of his surroundings. *Would Helen want to live in such conditions?* He obviously was not a man of great means, nor would ever be if he continued on his current course as a minister, so would such a life be acceptable to her?

He had not even thought about that, possibly because this life seemed so unreal to him, as if he were walking in someone else's shoes. It would seem more reasonable for him to believe he was a wealthy man instead of someone who was used to doing without.

He realized he never fully discussed his background with Helen. Perhaps she could fill in the missing information and provide insight on his exact status in life. If he had money, where was it and how was he to get it? He thought about writing his mother about it, but then he would have to explain about his lapse in memory.

There seemed to be no solutions in sight.

The strange, foreign feelings he'd been experiencing all morning only increased when he pulled on the plain cotton shirt and britches he'd been given by one of the church members. They were slightly tight around his broad shoulders and a tad long in the leg, but it was the quality that made it seem so odd. If he lived and helped out on a farm, wouldn't he be used to dressing like this?

How he wished he could find just one answer.

He walked around the cloth that divided his room from the living area. There was a basket of food items set on the table, and the only thing he could manage to eat, since it required no cooking skills, was the plums.

The rest of the bag contained rice, potatoes, dried beans, and a few jars of figs, which North instinctively knew he did not like.

Since his stomach was growling, he knew that he was left with only one choice: He would have to go out and gather some eggs and get milk from the cow. Then, of course, he'd have to figure out how to actually cook the eggs.

Taking a deep breath for fortitude, North stepped out of the house, walked across his front porch, down the steps, then behind the house to the small barn.

The first thing that greeted him was the cow. She had such a baleful look on her face, as though she were afraid he was about to have her butchered. North decided right then and there the cow would be called Queen Mary, after Mary, Queen of Scots, because he had an idea that is what the martyred queen's face must have looked like when she was being led to her execution!

"Look here," he spoke to the wary cow. "I don't have the slightest idea what I'm about, so if you'll be patient with me and let me take some of your milk, I'll let you have all the grass you can eat. Do we have a deal?"

Queen Mary continued to stare at him without so much as a blink. "Come on, give over, old girl," he urged as he patted the coarse hair on her back. This time the cow just turned her massive head away from him and let out a long breath. "Hmm, not very trusting, I see."

"Are you expecting her to just hand over her milk in a bucket?" a young voice asked from the doorway. Embarrassed, North jerked around to find Josie and Helen standing there smiling at him.

"How long have you two been standing there?" he asked carefully.

"Long enough to see you know nothing about farm animals," Josie answered, only to receive a nudge from Helen.

"Josie, don't be indelicate," Helen scolded.

North held out his hand. "No, don't correct her, for she is right. I fear that I will starve for my lack of animal husbandry knowledge."

Helen and Josie giggled at his pitiful expression. "You won't this morning!" Helen told him, holding up a cloth-covered basket that smelled delightful. "We have brought fresh muffins and milk, so your . . . uh . . . Queen Mary, is it? Your Queen Mary will not have to be bothered this morning."

Hunger overcame any embarrassment North might have been feeling. He quickly led them to the benches under his oak tree. It wasn't until he had finished off two of the muffins that he was able to talk.

"These are quite delicious!" he complimented with a satisfied sigh as he reached over to take another.

"I knew you would like them. Christina told me you once ate a whole plate of them," Helen told him, as she brushed the crumbs from her light pink skirt. Today she was clad in a short-sleeved cotton day dress, and her hair was tied back with a matching pink ribbon. It was a simple gown suited for the hot, humid weather that also suited Helen's beautiful, creamy skin, black lash-framed eyes, and pink lips.

His ears perked up at hearing a name she had not mentioned before. "Christina? Who is she?"

There was a stillness that came over Helen that North did not understand. It was as though she had said something she shouldn't, yet it didn't make sense. How did Christina fit into both their lives?

"She is a girl I grew up with," she answered vaguely and quickly. She then jumped up from her seat and said in an edgy tone, "I have an idea! Since I grew up on a farm, I could show you how to milk the cow." She started walking toward the barn. "There is no time like the present," she yelled over her shoulder.

North didn't know what to think of her behavior. Confused, he looked at Josie, and the young girl just shrugged. "She only becomes nervous and does crazy things when you're around, you know," she explained in a conspiratorial whisper. "The rest of the time she is extremely proper and concerned at all times about being a lady."

Hmm. Interesting. Perhaps Helen liked him as much as he liked her.

That didn't explain the evasiveness about her friend Christina, though.

"Let's go learn to milk a cow, shall we?" he asked Josie as he extended his hand to her.

Josie, clearly not thrilled by that prospect, rolled her eyes and sighed. "Oh, all right. But I'm almost sure this is not on the list of ladylike duties I have to learn."

North laughed as he led her to the barn. "No, probably not."

How could I be so careless? Helen lamented, as she paced back and forth in the barn. The more information she offered, the more he was going to want to know, and the more lies she would have to tell.

Oh, this was truly the most awful idea she had ever schemed! Once North found out how much she deceived him and concealed from him, he would never want to see her again! Last night she had tried to tell him the truth, but he wouldn't listen. And she couldn't tell him now because Josie was with her.

Helen was caught in a web of her own making, one that was created for the cause of love but was truly selfish at its very core. All because she wanted something she couldn't have.

"We're here for our lesson!" North announced cheerfully as he and Josie dashed through the barn door, startling the cow and upsetting the three chickens sitting over in the corner.

Helen looked at the cow and wished she hadn't been so hasty in her suggestion. Though she'd seen cows being milked a dozen or so times by her father's servants, she'd never actually milked one herself. "Well . . . ," she sounded, stretching the word out as she thought of what to do. "We need a bucket, but I don't see one."

Josie snatched a bucket that was hanging from a nail on the wall beside her. "I found one!"

"Wonderful," she replied, trying to sound confident as she took the bucket from her charge. "Well, now we need a stool."

"Like the one there beside the cow?"

North asked. Helen looked keenly at him to see if he was on to her, but she couldn't tell whether he was teasing her or not.

"Uh, yes. There it is." She slowly edged her way to the side of the cow, praying the animal would not be difficult. She carefully sat down and stared with much apprehension at the cow's underparts in front of her.

She was going to have to touch the animal for this to work, and she didn't want to touch it at all. She remembered petting a cow once, but that was the extent of it. She had never touched the underbelly of one.

She glanced back at North, who had come to stand behind her, and once again, he seemed truly interested in what she was doing. "Are you all right?" he asked when she looked back at the cow and then to him once more.

"Oh, yes . . . yes . . . I am fine. I just wanted to make sure you were paying attention," she answered.

"You have my full concentration," North assured.

"Capital, just capital!" she murmured between gritted teeth. Taking a deep breath, she slowly reached out and took hold of the cow. The cow stirred a little, but that was all.

She tried to pull like she had seen the

servant do, but no milk came out.

"Trouble?" North asked.

Helen ignored him as she pulled again, and still nothing. Three, four, then five times she tried but only succeeded in making the cow become irritable.

Finally she couldn't take it anymore. Helen jumped up from her seat, causing the stool to fall back, the cow to move around, and the chickens to be once again upset.

"I don't think she's in the mood to be milked," Helen said quickly, as she brushed at her skirt, then tried to push a few stray hairs away from her face.

North folded his arms and appeared to study the cow. "I wasn't aware that cows needed to be in the mood."

"Yeah, I've never heard that, either," Josie added. "Are you sure you've milked a cow before?"

Putting her hands on her hips, Helen held her chin up with as much bravado as she could muster. "Actually, no. But I've seen it done plenty of times." She tapped her fingertip on her hips. "Enough to know when a cow is in the mood to be milked or not!"

North narrowed his gaze at her, but she could see the humorous gleam shining in his eyes. "So how do I know when she's in the mood?"

Helen suddenly realized he'd known all along she was faking it. She pointed her finger at him and charged, "Why didn't you tell me you were on to me? You actually let me touch that . . . that . . . thing!"

Both Josie and North were doubled over laughing by this point. "I can't wait . . . to see how . . . you do . . . with the chickens!" he said between laughs.

Helen smiled confidently as she marched over to one of the hens and deftly slipped her hand under the chicken and quickly withdrew it, holding an egg triumphantly in the air. "Now let's see you try," she challenged, knowing what the outcome would be to a novice.

Just as she thought would happen, North walked over to the hen, poked and prodded through its feathers and, instead of an egg, got a painful peck on the wrist for his efforts.

"Oh, dear," she said with mock innocence. "I fear you did not do that correctly."

North frowned as he rubbed his hand. "I take it you've done this before?"

"Many times."

North grinned at her, and her heart did a flip-flop. To finally have all his attention directed at her, after many months of having him be merely polite to her while she pined away for him every time she saw him, was a heady experience indeed. The sight of him being so natural and at ease, standing in a barn surrounded by chicken feathers and a smelly cow, made her wish he were truly who he thought he was — a simple preacher.

While it was true that North was always a very nice man despite his exalted position in society, he always seemed to be aware of and took care with everything he did — every move he made. He seemed bound by the dictates of his society and the boundaries of the English society, or the ton, as they were called.

Now he didn't have those restrictions on him. There was no one watching how he dressed or with whom he kept company. There were no responsibilities on him since he didn't realize that he had the burden of taking care of four estates and watching after his many investments, not to mention the people who depended on him for their livelihood. He thought he was simply a country preacher whose only worry at the moment was probably the sermon he would have to preach on Sunday and how to get his cow to give milk.

Despite his confusion, he seemed relaxed

and content.

Because of his confusion, there was nothing keeping him from hiding his interest in her. There was nothing keeping him from smiling at her and looking at her as though she was the most important person to him.

But that doesn't make it right, said a tiny voice, which she knew was the conviction of God nudging at her heart. He deserved to know who he was. His cousins deserved to know that their family member was still alive and well.

"Shall we begin again?" he asked, breaking her from her musings. "Perhaps if we three put our heads together, we can figure out how to milk this cow."

Laughing, Helen agreed, and so did Josie. Of course, the younger girl was up for anything that kept her from her lessons.

For about an hour, they worked on the poor cow. They finally got some milk out of her, but Helen had a strong suspicion that it was because the animal got tired of their pulling and prodding!

The difficult part, however, was dodging North's probing questions and her trying to answer without actually lying. "So Christina is married to a man named Nicholas who is a former soldier?" He repeated what she'd just told him, and Helen could tell that he was trying to see if the names were familiar to him.

"Nicholas and Christina are the Earl and Countess of Kenswick, you know," Josie informed him, much to Helen's dismay. She'd forgotten all about telling her of them. She quickly looked at North to see if he recognized any of these names.

North's brow furrowed as he stood up from his seat by the cow. "They're nobility?" he asked curiously, and Helen couldn't help but breathe a sigh of relief that his thoughts had taken a different direction from what she imagined he was thinking.

"Yes," Helen affirmed as she walked over to the chickens and finished gathering their eggs. "Christina is only a vicar's daughter, but Nicholas fell in love with her despite the ton's objections."

"Ah, you tell the story with a wistful sound in your voice," he said with a grin. "I gather you thought the whole affair was sentimental and romantic."

She handed the eggs over to Josie, who ran out of the barn to take them to the house. "As a matter of fact, I did," she answered with a raised brow, challenging him to say something against her romanticism.

"I'll bet when the censure came from

England's society and his family, it did not feel quite as romantic as they dreamed it would be. Marrying against one's own class can cause a great deal of heartache for all involved." He stopped and blinked. "Well, I say! I don't know where that little insight came from!" he retorted with a chuckle.

Helen laughed in return, but it was a hollow gesture. If he felt that way now, he'd still hold to those convictions once he got his memory back, she realized. Perhaps North, as a duke, didn't want to shake up his life unnecessarily whether it was for love or not.

"I don't think that particular thing is something we have to worry about, do you?" he teased, but she could see the interest for her burning in his gaze as he looked at her. How she wished things could always be as they were now.

"We'd better get this milk stored to keep it cold," she said instead of answering his question.

If she thought North would not notice her evasiveness, she was wrong. As he picked up the bucket of milk, he gave her a long look that let her know she would not be able to avoid his questions forever.

CHAPTER 5

A loud knock awoke North the next morning, and with a jolt, he was sitting up in his bed, scrambling to get his bearings. His bleary eyes scanned the room, and he noticed that it wasn't even light outside yet.

Who in the world would be out at this early hour? Where were his servants, and why weren't they doing something about the loud noise?

Bit by bit, the fog of sleepiness lifted, and he remembered where he was. He remembered *who* he was . . . at least he remembered who everyone *told* him he was.

"Hamish Campbell. I am Hamish Campbell, the vicar of this hot, muggy spot of America." He recited this to himself to try to lift the odd confusion that had come over him since he'd awakened. For a moment . . . he felt different somehow. Not at all like Hamish Campbell, the humble, poor preacher of Golden Bay.

He remembered thinking that his servants would answer the door. He wondered why he would automatically think he had servants to see after him. Did he once have them in England and Scotland?

Once again, several loud raps sounded on his door. North grudgingly pulled himself out of bed and quickly donned his plain, wrinkled clothes.

When he finally opened the door, he was surprised to find a tall, slim, black man dressed in a fine brown suit with a darker brown-and-black-striped vest over a snow-white shirt and expertly tied cravat.

"*Bonjour,* Monsieur Campbell," the man greeted in a crisp, confident tone as he bent in a short bow. "I am Pierre LeMonde, a freedman from New Orleans and currently in the employ of Mr. Robert Baumgartner. I am versed in all manner of household chores and have been at Golden Bay to teach their household staff the correct methods in which to carry out their duties. I not only speak excellent English but also French, which is my first language."

Slightly bemused by the lengthy, confusing speech, North automatically responded to his last statement without any thought. "Bonjour, monsieur. *Heureaux pour vous rencontrer,*" he replied in French, telling him he was pleased to make his acquaintance.

"*Et vous aussi,*" Pierre answered, and North understood him to say that he was pleased to meet him, too.

But he didn't know *how* he knew this.

Would a simple preacher know this? Was this something one learned at seminary or university?

"I'm sorry, monsieur, but are you all right?" Pierre asked, bringing North's attention back to the present.

"I think I am a little unclear as to why you are here," he told him bluntly, still shaken from discovering yet another odd piece of the puzzle that didn't seem to fit in with what he knew of his life.

"Miss Helen Nichols informed her employers you were in need of . . . how shall I say . . . domestic help."

North grinned at the man's effort at being tactful. "She told you about the fiasco with the cow and chickens, did she not?"

Pierre put his hand against his mouth and let out a little cough. "Uh-hum. Well yes, monsieur, she did."

North laughed as he stepped back and motioned for the man to come into his small house. "I will take help any way I can get it, even if I have to promote my embarrassing moments to get it."

Pierre smiled broadly as he entered the house. He inspected the room and then quickly turned to look at North with the same critical eye. "You are not what I imagined you'd be," he said finally, his deep tone thoughtful.

Intrigued, North cocked his head to one side as he asked, "Why do you say that?"

Pierre shook his head as he shrugged his slim shoulders. "I have been in the employ of some of the richest families of south Louisiana. English, Spanish, and French — it does not matter. They all had the same quality about them, the same air. They spoke differently — they walked differently than the average man or woman." He motioned his hand in a sweeping gesture toward North. "You possess these same qualities."

North scampered to remember what Helen had told him. Did she say his family was or had been wealthy? Oh, yes. She had been very vague as to the exactness of his financial status. So instead he went with his intuition — what he felt deep in his heart. "I am from a wealthy family," he answered, praying it was not a lie.

Pierre lifted an eyebrow as he nodded his head slowly. "Then that explains it. And you gave up your comfortable life for God's calling," he reflected aloud. "Very noble."

If only he could feel the calling, North thought sadly. He must have felt the zeal that had caused missionaries and preachers through the centuries to leave their friends and family to do the work of God. All he felt was scared and uncertain about his ability to minister effectively to these American people.

"I'm just doing the will of God," he said to Pierre, and as he said it, he knew that statement to be true. Somehow, some way, God had a plan, and North was a big part of it.

"Then you are fortunate," Pierre told him, his face solemn. "There are many of my people here in this country who cannot be free to do work such as yours but are bound by the dictates of their masters."

North nodded. "It is indeed a travesty. I would think, however, you are not sitting idly by," he guessed, sensing Pierre would be one who worked behind the scenes, trying to help those slaves whom he could.

Pierre pretended to straighten the cuffs of his sleeves and nonchalantly answered, "I have no idea what you mean, monsieur."

At that moment, North heard his stomach growl, reminding him of his hunger. He started to ask Pierre if his talents extended to knowing how to cook when another knock sounded at the door. Shaking his head, North lamented, "Americans are certainly early risers!"

Pierre smiled as he breezed past North, heading for the door. "Allow me, monsieur."

This time there were two men at the door, and both were holding either end of a large trunk. Pierre spoke to them briefly, then turned back to North to inform him that these were men from the New Orleans port.

"Excellent!" North exclaimed. "Just put it on the table there." The men did as asked, and Pierre gave them water for the journey home.

After the men had gone, Pierre helped North bring the trunk into his small room and then, much to North's eternal thankfulness, left him to make breakfast.

North didn't open the trunk right away. For a moment, he stood there contemplating what the old, beat-up trunk might hold. Would there be mementos inside to help him remember? Would the smell of the clothes or the sound of the trunk's creaking hinges unlock the closed doors of his mind?

He put his hands on the scuffed metal that framed the lid and slid them over until they reached the latch. Carefully he lifted the lid and waited for something familiar to wash over him.

It never came.

It was a trunk filled with clothes that seemed as though they belonged to a stranger. There was nothing vaguely familiar about them. Not even the smell of them gave him the tiniest twinge of remembrance.

Disappointment struck North to his very soul as he slumped down on the bed, his shoulders bent in defeat. He wiped his hands down his face, then through his hair as he tried to assure himself it did not mean anything, that his mind just hadn't healed sufficiently to get his memory back.

Curiosity, however, soon overpowered his disappointment. North stood again and started sifting through the contents of the chest. Perhaps if he could not remember, he could at least try to piece together certain aspects of his life.

Underneath a small stack of neatly pressed white shirts, North found four very worn books. But when he saw the titles and the authors, he was more confused than ever. The first three were religion-based writings by Jonathan Edwards, an evangelist from the Great Awakening period in America, and John Wesley, the man responsible for starting the Methodist movement in England. Curious, North just stared at the books as he tried to comprehend the greater meaning behind his apparent choices in literature.

Was he a Methodist or part of the Church of England? North could not remember how he obtained the information, but he knew the Methodists in England were a religious people only just tolerated by society. The Church of England would not accept their teaching in their chapels and abbeys, so they would meet elsewhere, constructing their own buildings and oftentimes moving to America, where they could worship without censure.

North understood their ministers spoke passionately when they preached, which caused many to call them radical, or religious zealots. North was aware, however, he didn't feel this way about them but only felt a curiosity when he thought about it.

He truly wished he could remember what denomination he was! What if he taught something that this particular congregation did not agree with?

It was just one more thing he'd have to ask Helen about and pray that she knew something about it.

Setting those books aside, he then noticed the title of the fourth book, and he immediately smiled. Daniel Defoe's *Robinson*

Crusoe, he intuitively knew, was one of his favorite stories. Perhaps it may have been the catalyst to bringing him to America.

A shimmer of shining metal caught the corner of his eye, and he looked down to notice a gold frame peeking out from under a folded pair of britches. North set the Defoe book aside and reached for the frame.

As he got a better look at it, he saw it was a double-oval frame that contained two miniatures of a man and a woman. North concentrated all his energies into the study of the small portraits as he moved his gaze from the brown-haired man's eyes and smile to the pretty woman's red curls and delicate features.

It struck North right away that neither of them had blond hair. As a matter of fact, neither even looked like him.

North didn't know why this upset him, but it did. In fact, he was more affected by the miniatures than by any of the other disappointments he'd yet encountered.

Agitated, he gripped the frame and began to pace the room. Closing his eyes and gritting his teeth, he focused hard, trying to make his mind remember something . . . anything!

Absolutely nothing was achieved except

perhaps a headache from the pressure of trying.

Walking to his window, he pushed the light blue cotton curtain aside. His eyes focused on the church, which was situated in his direct line of view, and then he did the only thing he knew to do.

Pray.

"God, I cannot understand why I can't remember. I cannot understand why I become more confused looking at my own belongings. Most of all, I cannot understand why I don't feel like Hamish Campbell." He took a breath and lifted the miniature up to the sunlight. Thoughtfully he rubbed his thumb along the edges of the frame. "I can only conclude that You have a purpose, Lord, and need me to fulfill it. I will endeavor to feel honored You have chosen me for Your task, and please forgive me when I have felt otherwise since I arrived in Golden Bay. I will strive to do my best for You, dear God. Please help my faith to stay strong." He ended the prayer and stayed a minute more, gazing out the window, letting the heat of the sunlight bathe his face and rejuvenate his spirits.

In fact, he felt so much contentment in his heart that he wasn't even fazed when he tried on his clothes from the trunk and found the shoulders were just a little tight and the arms just slightly too long.

Apparently I had an atrocious tailor in Scotland was his only thought as he made his way to the kitchen and to the delicious food Pierre already had spread on the table.

"Josie, a lady never grabs the body of her teacup with both hands!" Helen stressed as she was unsuccessfully trying to tutor the young girl on the correct way to take tea.

Josie looked at Helen with a typically bored expression on her features. "Which would you prefer: my picking the cup up by the handle and dropping it, getting tea everywhere, or would you rather see me using both hands to make sure that doesn't happen?"

Considering the cost of the teacups they were using, the young lady had a point. But Helen couldn't tell her that.

"Josie, if you practice, you will be able to hold on to your cup without dropping it and look elegant at the same time," she instructed patiently, knowing Josie was barely paying attention. The younger girl kept looking out the window with a longing expression. She cleared her throat to get Josie's attention. "Shall we begin again?"

Josie sighed with vexation. "Why don't we

go visit the reverend and see how he's getting along? It's been over a week since we've seen him," she said, suddenly perking up.

Helen wanted more than anything to go but knew it was wiser to stay away. It was getting more and more difficult to live with the lie she had told him. Seeing him only compounded her guilt. "Josie, please . . . ," she began only to be cut short.

"Can't we go fishing instead? Sam is going to be there, and he was going to show me how to use crickets for bait."

Helen shuddered at her words. "Your fascination with that Indian is beyond the pale! Young ladies do not go traipsing around alone with young men who are not in one's family!"

Josie's chin rose, and Helen knew she wasn't going to back down. "You just don't like Sam because he keeps wanting to trade horses for you."

"Exactly! He is a barbarian!" In truth, Helen was a little fascinated with Sam, the tall, red-skinned man who dressed in his leather-fringed britches and only covered his upper torso with a closed vest, leaving his arms bare. It was even a little flattering he seemed so taken with her.

Josie slumped in her chair and folded her arms defiantly. "I should have been born an

Indian; then I wouldn't have to learn all these dumb rules."

Helen smiled. "I'm sure there are a whole different set of rules you would have to learn as an Indian girl."

Josie's rebuttal was stopped short when her mother breezed into the room at that moment. "I just received a note from Pierre that all is going well at the Reverend Campbell's house," she informed them as she waved a small piece of paper in her hand.

Helen stood and looked at her employer gratefully. "Thank you so much for sending help," she told her earnestly. "I saw he was unfamiliar with animals and even how to prepare his own meals, so I feared he would starve without immediate assistance."

Imogene raised an eyebrow as she studied Helen with a critical eye. She made Helen feel like the woman could see straight inside her mind. "I see I was right in my assumptions."

Helen could feel her heart beating with nervousness. "I beg your pardon?" she said, hoping she was misreading the direction of Mrs. Baumgartner's thoughts.

"You have feelings for Hamish Campbell!" she declared with certainty. "Your eyes light up when you speak of him, and an inner joy exudes from your heart and into your words. I would even be so bold as to say that you were in love with the reverend even before you came to Louisiana. Am I right?"

Helen tried to swallow the lump in her throat, but she was so frozen by what she should say next, she was unable to accomplish the task. She said the first thing she thought of, hoping her words would defuse Imogene's assumptions. "I can honestly say that I am not in love with Hamish Campbell." She was only in love with Trevor "North" Kent.

She must have sounded convincing, because Imogene frowned with confusion. "Are you absolutely sure?" she asked but then continued without an answer. "Perhaps you have not realized your feelings for him yet! Of course!" She clapped her hands together. "You need time to sort them out!"

Did a girl really need time to realize that she had found her true love? The moment Helen had laid eyes on North, she knew he was the only man she wanted to be her husband, the only man she could love.

"You can only be sure of your feelings if you spend time with him!" She patted Helen on the cheek and spun around to walk toward the door. "Don't worry, dear! Leave it to me. You'll realize he is your one true love in no time!" she exclaimed over her shoulder as she left the room.

Bemused by Mrs. Baumgartner's words, Helen could only liken the feeling to being run over by a buggy.

"You may be good with manners and such, but you are wretched at handling my mother," Josie spoke from behind her as Helen still stood staring at the door.

Blinking, Helen finally turned and looked at the younger girl. "I don't suppose you can give me any pointers on how I should do that, can you?"

Josie's smile was one of pure cunning. "Only if I can go fishing with Sam today."

Plopping back down in her chair, Helen waved her hand toward the door. "Just go," she told her in a tired voice, and in just a matter of seconds, the girl had flown out of the room and down the stairs.

Helen thought about all that had transpired since she had arrived in Louisiana and wondered if things could become any stranger. Here she was in love with a man who had no memory and whom everyone believed was someone else. She was trying to hide the fact that she was in love with him, but now Imogene Baumgartner was determined to see them together.

Why am I fighting this? Helen thought, but deep down she knew the answer. Guilt was holding her back. Guilt over lying to poor North about who he really was.

The whole purpose of making him think he was Hamish Campbell was to have a chance at winning his heart. But even if he never got his memory back, could she live with such a lie hanging over her head? Could she even keep up the charade without anyone finding out?

She imagined telling the vicar from her village, the Reverend Wakelin, about her deceptive deeds and wondered what he would say. Helen knew he would be very disappointed in her, because she was growing more and more ashamed of herself.

Chapter 6

"Pierre!" North called out as he entered his house, holding a basket of eggs. He'd been in Golden Bay nearly two weeks now, and dealing with the animals was still a daily challenge. "I got out every single egg without damaging myself in the process!" he announced proudly as he put the basket on the table.

Pierre peered over his shoulder as he knelt in front of the fireplace, where he was adjusting the metal rack mounted inside. "Very good, monsieur. Perhaps tomorrow you will be able to get a little more than half a cup of milk from the cow."

North laughed at Pierre's droll tone. "Could you let me savor my small victory before criticizing my failures?"

"I am just helping you to strive for more, monsieur," Pierre countered with laughter in his deep voice.

"Well, I am about to strive to write my

first sermon, so if you'll excuse me, I'll go and get my Bible."

"It is Saturday!" Pierre exclaimed with disbelief. "You are only now preparing your sermon?"

North stopped in his tracks and looked to Pierre with concern. "That's not the way it's done?" he asked cautiously, not thinking about his words.

Pierre blinked at him and paused a minute before asking, "You don't know?"

North felt like a fraud. Here he was pretending to be the person he really was . . . except he couldn't remember being that person. And if everyone knew he couldn't remember, then they would either think he was crazy or doubt his ability to lead them.

Which would be a proper assumption in his case because he had no idea how to be a vicar and no inkling as to whether he was even good at public speaking. Maybe the reason he came all the way to America was because everyone back in Scotland thought he was a terrible preacher.

"Uh . . . my experience has been somewhat . . . limited," he finally answered with the biggest understatement of the decade.

Pierre's right eyebrow rose in query. "How limited?"

"Practically nonexistent."

Pierre just stared at him for a moment, making North wonder what he was thinking. Would he go tell the Baumgartners that he was a fraud? A novice who had no business pretending he knew *anything?*

Then Pierre suddenly turned from him, and his shoulders began to shake. North peered closely at him, and when he'd walked to face Pierre once again, he realized the man was laughing!

"I'm sorry, monsieur, but you English are very funny," he said, as tears started to run down his dark cheeks. "I wish I could be in that church tomorrow. It would be more —" He interrupted his own sentence as he tried desperately to hold on to his usual dignified disposition. "More entertaining than watching you milk that poor . . . cow!"

North sighed as he watched Pierre sit down at the table and completely cover his face as his whole body shook.

North wished he could see the humor of the whole situation. He could use a good laugh.

Leaving the still-laughing servant in the kitchen, North dragged his feet into his bedroom and took the Bible from his night table. He opened the book at random, praying for divine intervention, and landed in the book of Exodus. He read the story about how Moses led the children of Israel out of Egypt and how their disobedience kept them in the desert, which should have taken them a short time to go through, for forty years.

He sat there for a moment and thought about how that story could be used in a sermon, but then he had a horrible thought. What if he had done some incredibly bad thing or had been disobedient to God before he came to America? Perhaps God was punishing him for this.

Perhaps he would be stuck in a wilderness of forgetfulness for forty years like the children of Israel!

Looking back down at the faded pages of the Bible, North quickly flipped the pages away from that particular book. He decided it would be best to look for something else.

He looked through several passages, and none seemed to be right for his first sermon until he found the book of Job. Here was a man who had lost everything but still would not blame God for any of his misfortunes. And in time, God restored him above and beyond his former glory because Job stayed faithful to God.

North rubbed his chin as he thought about how Job's life was similar to his own. Everything had been stripped from him, so if he continued to keep his faith in God, perhaps He would restore to North what he had lost.

He determined he would build his sermon around the story of Job. North felt that since he was so affected by the story he would have the passion to convey the lesson to others.

Encouraged that he had a theme for his message, he took several sheets of paper from his trunk and went to the kitchen with pen and ink in hand.

"You look pleased with yourself," Pierre observed. "I will assume it is because you have found a theme for your sermon?"

"Yes, you may assume," North said with a relieved smile. "I am speaking about the life of Job and how we should keep our faith in God when things go wrong in our lives."

Pierre looked impressed. "An excellent topic. How will you begin?"

North thought a moment. "I will open by reading the scriptures." He opened his bottle of ink, situated his papers just so, and dipped the tip of the pen into the bottle.

"And then?"

North looked up as Pierre sat across from him. He had on the same suit as yesterday, and North couldn't help but notice his own servant dressed better than he did.

"Then . . . I will put the story into my own words — explain it, if you will."

He began to write down the scripture reference in his bold, yet expertly done, script.

"Ah . . ." Pierre sounded thoughtful. "And where shall you go from there?"

North smudged his paper when his hand jerked at Pierre's words. "I should have more?" Suddenly the process seemed complicated again.

"*Oui,* monsieur. What you've described will take less than seven to ten minutes. It will need to be a great deal longer than that."

North looked from the near-empty paper to Pierre with dismay radiating from every pore of his being. "I don't suppose you could . . ."

Pierre made a *tsk*-ing sound. "I write very poorly, monsieur. And besides, if I do it for you, it would not be from your heart but mine."

North sighed and ran a hand through his wavy blond hair. "Yes, I suppose you're right," he conceded, although he wished he knew what to do.

Helen suddenly came to mind, and he wondered if she could help him. Of course she had been to church before, so perhaps she could give him an idea of what to do. And besides, she was the only person who would understand *why* he didn't know what to do.

He quickly gathered his papers and put the top back on his ink. "May I borrow your barouche, Pierre?"

Pierre seemed taken aback by his sudden change. "Of course, but why?"

"Because I'm going to see Helen. She'll be able to help me."

Pierre helped him don his coat and put his things in a leather satchel, which North had found near the bottom of the trunk. "Perhaps there are other reasons you want to see the pretty lady?"

"Mind your own affairs, Pierre," he ordered as he walked briskly to the door.

He heard Pierre shout as he closed the door. "But yours are so much more interesting than my own!"

North's heart was beating excitedly as he knocked on the Baumgartners' door. Just the prospect of seeing Helen once again seemed to reduce him to a nervous schoolboy with his first crush.

Of course, since he couldn't remember even going to school, she would actually be the first.

A tall black man dressed in fine black attire greeted North with a solemn nod and asked him the reason for his visit.

Before he could answer, Imogene Baumgartner came hurriedly down the staircase to greet him. "Reverend Campbell! How wonderful you have come to visit us."

They both nodded to each other in lieu of a curtsy or bow. "Good morning, Mrs. Baumgartner. I came by to see if I might have a word with Helen."

North was surprised to see the older woman's eyes light up. "Of course you did!" she exclaimed as she put a hand against her throat and looked at him as if she knew a secret. "Our Helen is a very special lady, if I might be so bold as to say." She leaned forward and whispered, "But I think you are already aware of that."

North was well aware Imogene Baumgartner was not a lady of high society. Pierre had told him about her being the daughter of a servant in England and that Robert Baumgartner had given up everything to marry her. But despite her obvious lack of ladylike behavior, she was a very engaging woman who quickly endeared herself to all those she met.

Again, North had no idea how he understood the differences of society and their behaviors. He couldn't even remember if he'd been considered a gentleman or simply a rich commoner. And there was a difference. Whereas a gentleman was born to his distinction whether he was wealthy or poor, a commoner, no matter how rich, could never hope to be recognized on the gentleman's level.

In America, however, it seemed that whoever had the most money or the drive to better themselves could achieve anything they wanted.

So North supposed it didn't really matter what he was, as long as he worked hard to establish himself and proved himself worthy to be called a minister to the Golden Bay people.

North smiled at Imogene, leaned forward, and whispered back to her, answering her assumption. "You are correct. I think Helen Nichols is a very lovely girl."

Imogene giggled with girlish delight, and North smiled with her, enjoying the merriment dancing in her light hazel eyes. "Why don't you wait right here in the library while I go and tell her you are here." She directed him to a small room off their grand foyer, just beyond the staircase.

North remained standing after she had left and looked with startled interest about the room. It was indeed a library with shelves made of what looked like heavy oak, but there were no more than twenty books spread about them as they circled the room. The rest of the space was taken up by potted plants, figurines, and a few miniatures.

"It seems sort of an atrocity to call this room the library, doesn't it?"

North turned toward the female voice that he was coming to recognize so well. He took a moment to admire how Helen had left her dark curls to flow around her shoulders, complementing the light violet of her morning dress. "Indeed, it is," he agreed. "It seems to be nothing but old books of poetry, scientific works, and . . ." His voice drifted to a pause when he noticed a stack of books in one far corner that seemed to be newer than the rest. "What are those over there?"

Helen smiled. "Those are mine. I'm afraid I wasted a lot of time in England reading and not applying myself to other studies as I should have."

Suddenly a thought popped into his head, and North spoke it without realizing what he was saying. "Of course! I remember you like to read gothic romance novels; am I correct?"

The moment those words were out, they

both froze — staring at one another in unbelief.

"How do you know that?" she finally asked, her voice sounding almost fearful.

North shook his head in wonderment. "I don't know. The information just appeared in my mind like a memory normally does."

"Well, do you remember anything else?"

North closed his eyes and tried to concentrate on the memory he just had but could remember nothing else. He opened his eyes and sighed. "Absolutely nothing."

Helen looked at him with sympathy. "I'm sorry, North. I'm sure more memories will come to you. Perhaps if you try not to think about it so much, you will one day remember everything."

"I suppose you're right," he readily agreed. It just felt so good for that tiny moment to have a true memory of something. It was like God giving him a small gift to get him through the day.

"What's that in your hand?" Helen prompted as she spied the satchel he had taken from his shoulder.

"Ah yes." He'd almost forgotten his reason for being here. "I've come to ask for your help with my sermon." He dipped his hand into the satchel and brought out his papers. "Since I can't remember preaching or even hearing a sermon, I don't have the first idea how to go about constructing one."

He watched as Helen smiled prettily and crossed her arms in front of her in a motion of confidence. "Well, Reverend, you've come to the right person!"

Helen was still a little jittery after North told her about his memory. Sure, it was a tiny memory, but who knew what he would remember next?

This was bad — very, very bad. *She* was bad for even creating this situation. But what could she do? If she told him now, it would not only confuse him but also upset the whole town!

She was trying to calm her nerves when he asked her the one thing that would help take her mind off her problem.

He needed help with his sermon. She could do that!

Helen motioned for North to sit at the desk by the far wall, and she pulled a chair beside him. "Can I assume you have a little knowledge in the area of sermon writing?" North asked as he reached over to take a Bible down from the shelf behind him.

"My best friend's father is a vicar. Every Saturday Christina and I would take his notes in his very sloppy script and rewrite them so that he could see them better from the pulpit," she explained. "I know exactly the structure in which he wrote all his sermons. They would have one major scripture reference and at least three points. At the end, he would bring it all together and bring out one last nugget of truth, maybe other scriptures in the Bible that might tie in with his first one. He was a very respected and widely known vicar in our parish."

North seemed surprised by her information. "You don't know how relieved I am that you seem confident in how to do this." He paused for a moment. "Uh . . . Helen, this congregation here in Golden Bay . . . Are they a Methodist congregation? That is to say . . . am I a Methodist?"

Helen shrugged her shoulders. "Actually, it is a sort of blended church. There are a few Methodists, Baptists, and members of the Church of England, as the Baumgartners and I are. I'm almost certain you are, as well." Actually she was *very* certain he was, but she'd already told him that she knew little about his personal life.

For over an hour, they labored side by side, working with his passage from Job and choosing points that best brought out the lesson he wanted to be most understood.

When they had finished, he leaned back

in his chair and stretched his arms forward. "I think I could use some fresh air," he said with a yawn.

Helen thought about how humid it had been outdoors earlier when she'd stepped out for a moment, and she smiled. "I don't know if *fresh* is the appropriate description of the Louisiana air, but I do concede that it would be nice to walk around a bit."

Together they stepped out onto the porch, which wrapped around the house, and made their way down the ten or so steps, following the path to the pier.

"So what caused you to leave England and journey to this place?" North asked as he picked up a long, thick stick from the path and then used it as a walking cane.

There was no way Helen could tell him the truth — that she'd come to America because she had hoped to see him. "Well, I suppose it sounded adventurous," she answered, giving him only half the truth. "My best friend had gotten married, and I suppose I just wanted a change of setting. My parents were hinting around for me to marry a young farmer in my village, and I just didn't want to settle for someone I didn't love." She shrugged her shoulders. "When Lady Claudia told me about the position of being a companion for her little sister, I felt God was opening a door for me. So here I am."

"Well, might I be so bold as to say I am eternally grateful that you did not settle for the farmer, or else I might have never seen you again," he said in a teasing tone as he looked down at her with appreciation.

Helen could feel her cheeks reddening, and she quickly looked away before he could read her true feelings. She knew he liked her, but it would be hard to explain the feelings of love she carried for him so soon.

North, however, was adept at stemming the awkwardness as he changed the subject to her earlier comment about Lady Claudia. She was trying to explain that Claudia, Robert Baumgartner's elder child, had been accepted by her grandfather to inherit the title of marchioness after his death, when something large moved in their path, blocking the sun.

Helen knew, before she lifted her gaze, who it was.

Standing before them with all the confidence a chief of his tribe would possess — wearing his usual buckskins and vest — was the Choctaw Indian Sam Youngblood. In his hand were three ropes that led to the horses situated behind him.

Helen could sense the moment North noticed him, and after a period of stunned silence, he barked out, *"What* is *that?"*

CHAPTER 7

Helen glanced back and forth between the two men nervously; and if she were pressed to describe their first reaction to one another, it would most definitely be *hostile.* Even *that* would be an understatement.

As soon as the words had left North's mouth, Helen feared Sam would surely take offense. And if his flaring nostrils and narrowed, angry eyes were any indication, Helen knew she was right in her assumption.

Realizing she would have to try and unruffle the Indian's feathers, so to speak, she began to walk toward him. Helen had only taken two steps when she was suddenly jerked back by North and pulled to his side.

"What are you doing? That is a savage!" North barked, sounding as though he were horrified at even being in Sam's presence.

Knowing how Sam usually liked to play up to people's stereotypical thinking that all

Indians were uneducated, barbaric, and dangerous, Helen knew he was probably already thinking of what to do to shock North even more.

"But, North, he's . . ."

"They've been known to scalp a fellow before he could even let out a scream," he stressed in a low voice, all the while keeping his eye on Sam. "They also like to take white women back to their camps and use them as their slaves."

Helen stopped short of rolling her eyes. "You know this, but you can't remember your own name," she whispered back with exasperation. Then in a louder voice, "North, if you'll just let me intro—"

"Why don't we start walking toward the house very slowly? Perhaps he'll leave us alone." He started to pull her to walk around Sam, when the Indian suddenly pulled out the long knife that had been strapped to his hip.

As Sam made a show of examining his blade, flashing the metal against the sunlight, Helen noticed North appeared to be growing more apprehensive by the minute.

"All right, you've had your fun, Sam. Now put the knife away," she called out.

Sam scowled at her. "But I haven't even shown him my frightening war cry," he complained.

North looked at her with disbelief. "You *know* him?"

Helen's arm was starting to hurt as North unconsciously kept tightening his grip. "If I vow with all sincerity that he will not scalp us, will you let go of my arm?"

North immediately let go, his face matching the apology he offered her. "Please accept my forgiveness; I did not realize . . ."

"Are you hurting my woman?" Sam roared angrily, as he stomped over to where they were standing.

Helen groaned, holding out a hand to stop the tall man. "Will you cease calling me your woman?" she lamented. "I've told you time and time again that —"

"I demand to know what he means by the words 'my woman'," North interjected, his question directed to Helen but his eyes steady on Sam.

Helen put her hands on either side of her face and shook her head. "Oh, dear! This is getting dreadfully out of hand. If you both would stop and listen —"

"I have tried three times to barter a trade between myself and Baumgartner for Helen," Sam started to explain in his blunt way.

"You've done *what?*" North interrupted,

but Sam, unfazed, continued.

"He has rejected all my offers, but this time I don't think he will." He waved a hand back toward the black horses. "This time I have brought not two, but three of the finest horses around this area. I do not think he will refuse."

"Trade . . ." North choked as he listened to Sam. "That is the most preposterous thing I have ever heard. You can't be serious," he barked and turned to Helen. "Tell me he isn't serious."

"Sam, I told you our people do not trade women or even men for horses or anything else! It's just simply not civilized."

Sam scoffed at her words, which he'd heard many times before. "I have seen white men barter for the black men and women," he countered. "I see no difference!"

How can I argue with that? Helen stared at Sam, disconcerted. "Sam, I am not for sale, and there is no more I can say about it. Mr. Baumgartner, even if he wanted to, could not trade me to you. He doesn't own me."

"I can't even believe I am hearing this conversation. Why are you trying to reason with him?" North said, exasperation threaded in his tone.

"This is none of your business, white

man!" Sam barked, his eyes glaring at North.

Helen quickly jumped in, in an attempt to defuse whatever was happening between the two mistrustful men. "I haven't introduced you two, have I?" she asked brightly as she stepped between them, causing them both to back up. "This is Sam Youngblood, Reverend Campbell. He lives just across the bayou. Sam, this is my friend, North. He is the new preacher in town."

Suddenly the hostility left Sam's face, and he smiled broadly. "You are a preacher?"

North seemed unsure of how to react to the Indian's sudden change of attitude. "Yes," he answered after a brief pause.

Sam nodded as he zeroed in his focus on Helen, his interest in her shining in his dark, mysterious eyes. "That's good. Because if I can't barter for Helen, then I suppose I'll have to get her another way," he stated.

North tried to move around Helen, but she kept sidestepping him. Finally he just pointed to Sam over her shoulder. "And what other way would that be?"

Helen moaned, "Oh, dear!" She looked over her shoulder and saw Sam was actually enjoying the fact he was upsetting North.

Sam shrugged, and with a sigh that sounded as though he was quite put out, he answered, "I'll have to woo her into marrying me, I guess."

"Mar—" North choked on his words again. "Did you hear what he just said?" he practically shouted at her.

Oh yes, she'd heard, and she was just a little perturbed at his seeming reluctance to try to court her. It didn't matter that she didn't want him to!

"You don't have to seem as though it would be a great hardship to woo me!" she scolded Sam. "You were certainly willing to give up your best three horses for me, so what is the difference?"

North, standing behind her now, tapped her on the shoulder and whispered forcibly in her ear, "Helen, do you hear what you are saying?"

"It's a lot less work!" Sam answered over North's whisper.

"Well, I never!" Helen huffed, insulted by his words.

"So can you marry us?" Sam asked over her shoulder to North, ignoring Helen's outrage.

"Absolutely not!" North stated with a steely resolve.

"I never said I would marry you!"

"Why not?" Sam pressed, his question not directed at her but at North again.

"I am not marrying anyone, so please stop discussing a wedding that will never happen!" she yelled at them both as she backed away and glared with hands on hips.

"Do you always yell like this? I'm not sure I want a wife who is so loud," Sam observed with a sudden frown.

Helen tapped her fingers on her hips. "Then I shall make sure to yell at you every time we meet!"

Sam scowled at that answer. North smiled at her with admiration.

Both men were driving her crazy.

Without so much as another word, she whirled around, tossing her dark curls behind her, and marched to the house.

North watched Helen flounce away, and he couldn't help but admire her spunk and the way she had stood up to Sam. She would indeed make a fine wife, but not to the Indian. No, she would make a very fine wife for a man like himself.

At least the man he imagined he was, he amended, as he thought about how his own past was still a mystery.

"So I have competition for Helen Nichols," Sam commented, as though he already knew the answer.

North answered anyway. "No, because you

have no chance in winning her heart." It was an overconfident statement for which he had nothing to back it up except his own hopes for Helen.

Sam stared at him as if he were trying to decipher the truth. "You believe you do?"

North smiled a confident smile filled with determination. "I know I do."

North returned the Indian man's stare measure for measure. Finally Sam answered with equal conviction, "We shall see, preacher man." And with that he nodded his head and turned to gather his horses.

As North began to walk back toward the path that Helen had taken, he realized he actually liked Sam, despite his fondness for the woman of North's choice. He found he looked forward to learning more about Sam's culture and way of life.

Did Indians of his tribe actually scalp people?

It wasn't hard to locate Helen after he'd reached the plantation house, because she was sitting on the front porch with Josie sipping tea. The first thing he noticed was that she'd tied back her beautiful black hair with a ribbon.

Pity.

"I was wondering if you two brutes had killed one another," she told him, as he walked up the many steps to where they were seated.

"Let's just say we had a few things to talk over," he prevaricated.

"Did he show you his big knife? I once saw him cut a snake clean in two with one swipe!" Josie threw in, apparently not wanting to be left out of the conversation.

"Never mind about that!" Helen waved toward the younger girl as if dismissing her words. "What possible things would you have to discuss with Sam?" she demanded to know.

North had to try hard not to smile at her curiosity. "I believe the subject revolved around" — he paused for effect — "your marriage."

"My *marriage!*" she gasped, coming out of her chair and nearly spilling the tea on the wooden floor.

"You're getting married?" Josie queried in an excited voice. "Who are you getting married to?"

"Nobody!"

"Wait and see."

They spoke at the same time, and Josie clapped her hands with delight. "I'll bet it's Sam! He's been in love with Helen since she got here!"

"But she's not in love with *him,*" North

answered without thinking, only realizing until after he spoke how self-assured he sounded.

One should never, ever presume to tell a woman what her feelings are, he remembered too late.

She gasped with incredulity at his words. North couldn't help but admire how beautiful she looked even when she was angry. "Perhaps I want to marry Sam!" she stated, emphasizing each word.

North knew good and well she didn't, but it didn't stop him from feeling irritated that she'd said it. "You've turned him down three times!" he countered with a snap of his fingers, remembering his earlier conversation with Sam.

Helen looked less angry, as if she thought she had the upper hand in the conversation. Almost deliberately she began to study her nails. "Maybe I was holding out for four horses."

The whole conversation seemed so silly that North began to laugh. A quick glance at Helen told him that she, too, found the whole exchange ridiculous. Soon they were both laughing.

"I don't know what is so funny," Josie huffed as she stood up from her chair. "If you don't want the horses, I'll take them!"

That just made them laugh harder.

CHAPTER 8

It was with great excitement that Helen and the Baumgartner family dressed for church the next morning. In fact, the whole area was abuzz with anticipation of finally having church services and their very own pastor. Weddings would not have to be delayed, and funerals could finally be done properly, with a minister presiding over them instead of someone just reading scriptures. There had been no one for spiritual guidance and no one qualified to go to for clarification on certain scriptures.

Among the females in the area, however, their excitement was not focused so much on the spiritual benefits but rather on the fact that he was young, single, and extremely handsome. Helen didn't really want to listen to that particular rumor from Imogene as they walked into the church, but there was plenty of evidence to support it when they entered and saw every female in the church dressed fancier than Helen had ever seen them.

Helen was amazed at the elaborately decorated bonnets that all seemed to match their frocks perfectly. It was almost like being transported back to London, so stylish they all looked. She glanced down at her own gown, which was nice with its pink flowers at the bodice and flowing cream taffeta below the high waist, yet it wasn't as stylish and well made as most of the dresses in the room. Even her bonnet, though one of her finest, seemed dowdy in comparison.

These were like all the society ladies whom North was used to being around in England. Would the sight of them jog his memory?

As she thought of North, she looked around but was unable to see him among the twenty or so people there in attendance. Helen took her seat beside the Baumgartners in one of the middle rows. It was then that she saw North enter the church from the side door by the pulpit.

She was only able to partially see his face as he took a seat in the front pew, and she wondered why he didn't look about the room at all. In fact, he seemed a little tense as he faced forward, not speaking to anyone.

Helen glanced to her side, and Josie, too,

seemed to be studying North's strange behavior. But before Helen could whisper anything to her young friend, Ollie Rhymes, the self-appointed hymn leader from the Hill plantation called for everyone to stand and turn to hymn number 23. It was then that Helen noticed the handmade booklet with words to songs written out in plain script and tied together with a heavy string. Since she was sitting on the end and there was only one booklet per pew, she was unable to sing the words to the unfamiliar song. It really didn't matter because poor Miss Ollie sang like an injured housecat, and since she was hard of hearing, her volume was one of gargantuan proportions.

Though Josie was all but holding her ears as she grimaced with mock pain, Helen barely gave Miss Ollie a glance, her gaze still fixed on North.

What is wrong with him?

"What's wrong with him?" Josie echoed her thoughts, talking louder than a whisper as she tried to make herself heard over the caterwauling.

Helen noticed the disapproving frown from Imogene directed at her daughter, so she just shook her head in lieu of an answer.

Finally Miss Ollie ended the song, and Helen could almost hear the audible prayer of thanks from everyone in the small church as the petite, elderly woman stepped down from the pulpit.

Miss Ollie smiled and nodded toward North, giving him his cue that it was his turn.

Apparently he didn't know the cue.

North just sat there, and after a few seconds, the congregation started whispering and moving around.

What *was* wrong with North?

Finally Miss Ollie apparently got tired of standing there and smiling at him. She went over to him, slapped him on top of his shoulder, and said, "It's your turn, sonny."

This time North responded with a jerk as if he had awakened from a dream. He quickly stood and looked around nervously. Stiffly, he walked to the pulpit and put down his Bible and notes.

It seemed like an eternity passed as he slowly flipped through his Bible, adjusted his papers, then cleared his throat at least four times.

"Has he ever done this before?" Josie whispered, still too loud. A smattering of laugher trickled from the people sitting around them as they heard her comment.

"Shh!" Helen sounded sharply as she prayed North would be able to calm down and begin his message.

Finally he read the scripture passage they'd chosen together. His voice sounded steady and strong as he read expertly from his Bible, and Helen started to relax.

He was doing fine. Of course, he could do this! He was, after all, a duke!

Unfortunately, poor North didn't have any idea who he was or what he was capable of. For after he read the scripture, he looked up at the crowd, looked back down at his Bible, and . . .

Nothing! He seemed unable to speak another word.

North was so seized with self-doubt that he couldn't seem to get another word out! He just couldn't seem to fathom why he had chosen the occupation of clergyman when he was so obviously afraid of speaking in public.

Wouldn't it be something that comes naturally? he wondered hurriedly as he struggled to get hold of his panic. But then nothing else had come naturally. Not taking care of animals, providing for himself without the help of a servant, and certainly not writing sermons. Why should he believe this would be any different?

Nothing felt right. His collar was too tight,

his shoes were actually a little too big, and he thought he might have gotten a splinter in his hand when he stepped up to the pulpit and ran his palm on the top of the wooden surface.

Read! Just read your message. It is all written out for you, he told himself so sternly that he feared he'd spoken it aloud. But when he looked at the congregation, they merely seemed curious and puzzled as to why he was just standing there, not saying anything.

He didn't want to tell them of his memory loss, because they would believe him to be crazy. If he didn't control his fear, they were going to come to that conclusion anyway!

Taking a deep breath, he prayed he would find a peace and be able to proceed. And miraculously God must have heard, because he was able to take a deep breath, his heartbeat slowing down so he could focus.

He lifted his gaze and saw Helen's concerned eyes fastened on him. A feeling like North knew he'd never felt before seemed to hit him square in the chest and straight to his heart. But it didn't make him more nervous; instead, it gave him a greater peace, knowing she was there to support him.

He smiled at her but quickly moved his

gaze about the room so as not to let anyone think he was flirting with a woman in church and in sight of everyone. When he briefly looked back at her, she was returning his smile, looking quite relieved that he seemed to be all right.

He looked back down at his notes and began to read. He kept trying to stop and make comments on what he was reading without having to look directly from his notes, but he couldn't seem to think of anything. So he read. And read.

And read.

He didn't *once* look up.

He finished the sermon in what he was sure was record time for a clergyman. In fact, the whole thing including the scripture reading could not have lasted more than ten minutes.

When he finally spoke the last words on his page, he looked up to find everyone staring at him with sort of a dazed expression on their faces. Not knowing what else to do, he quickly bowed his head and said a closing prayer, which sounded amateurish at best.

The members of his congregation were as polite as they could be as they filed out of the building, shaking his hand as they passed him. Every once in a while someone would actually tell him that his sermon was good, and North had to wonder if God wouldn't mind the lie so much since they were only trying to be nice.

Finally Helen was standing before him, giving him a smile that could only be described as one borne out of pity. *Splendid,* he thought grimly. The woman for whom he carried great affection felt sorry for him.

"You did it!" she whispered with encouragement. "It can only get easier from here."

North didn't feel quite so optimistic, but he did manage to murmur, "Thank you."

"You read really fast," Josie offered. She was wearing the same expression as Helen.

Helen nudged the younger girl and scolded, "Don't say that, Josie. He read quite nicely."

"I was trying to compliment him!"

North stemmed whatever Helen was about to say by stepping up and putting his hand on Josie's shoulder. "Thank you, Josie. You are very sweet," he told her, touched that she, too, was trying to help him feel better.

The sermon *really* must have been appalling.

"Reverend Campbell! Will you join us for our noonday meal?" Imogene asked, coming up behind Helen and Josie. "We have invited the whole church to come and picnic with us on our plantation."

There was nothing North wanted to do less than be around the congregation, but he saw no way to bow out graciously. "Of course I'll join you."

"Excellent!" Imogene exclaimed with a smile. "Then would you mind taking the barouche with Josie and Helen? I'll ride with my husband in our carriage."

He told her he would, and when everyone had exited the church, he closed it up and headed for the barouche, where Helen and Josie sat waiting for him.

Helen's face blossomed into a breathtaking smile when she saw him. North suddenly didn't care that he had embarrassed himself or that he would still have to face his congregation once again.

He was about to spend another day with Helen.

Nothing else mattered.

All through North's sermon, Helen couldn't help feeling responsible for putting him through the whole tedious ordeal. She felt such admiration for him because, even though he didn't know what he was doing, he was willing to give it his best efforts.

In fact, Helen realized now that she hadn't really known North at all back in England.

She had only been taken with his good looks and charming ways. She had never seen the giving, caring person who was nervous about public speaking and so determined to do what he thought was right — to be the man everybody thought he was even though he didn't feel like Hamish Campbell.

He was truly a good, decent man. A wonderful Christian man.

She didn't deserve him, but she couldn't tell him that. She couldn't tell him any of the truths she, and only she, knew to be true, because it would not only hurt him but everyone she respected in Golden Bay.

Helen felt terrible she had let things go this far. When she first thought of lying to him, she never stopped to consider the consequences. All of her reasoning was based on herself.

Now all she thought of was North. Every night she prayed not that God would forgive her but that He'd help her find a way of helping North get his memory back without hurting him too much in the process.

Unfortunately it sounded like an insurmountable task.

"All right, ladies. You are being too quiet, and Josie keeps smiling politely at me as if she's been instructed to do so," North said suddenly, breaking the long silence as they rode toward Golden Bay plantation. "Why don't you just give me your honest opinions? Trust me, it could be no worse than what I have already thought of myself."

"Well . . ." She hesitated, desperately trying to think of something positive to say. "You have a very nice voice for speaking. It's deep and very pleasant to listen to."

North threw her a look that told her he knew she was evading the question. "Wonderful! I read swiftly, and I have a pleasant voice. Anything else?"

"You could use some practice," Josie told him bluntly, making Helen groan with embarrassment. "Well, it is the truth, and that is what he asked for, isn't it?" she tried to reason after Helen glared at her.

"Josie, don't you remember our lesson on tact?" Helen stressed, then threw North an apologetic smile. "A lady does not voice every thought that pops into her mind!"

"Please don't scold, Helen," North interjected. "She is quite right. I do need practice."

Helen thought a minute about how the Reverend Wakelin prepared for his sermons. "If you start writing it tomorrow, perhaps by the time the week rolls by, it will become familiar to you. Perhaps it will help take away your nervousness and give you more confidence."

"Yes! And then you can practice your sermon on us!" Josie added excitedly. "We shall be your congregation, preparing you for the real one on Sunday."

North looked over at Helen, and she found herself moved by the appreciation that was radiating from his beautiful blue eyes. Her heart ached with all the love and affection that seemed to grow each time she was in his presence. There was a hope inside her that still refused to die.

A hope he really could love her and desire to marry her.

"Would you mind doing as Josie has suggested?" he asked, still holding her gaze as if he, too, could not look away. "I wouldn't want to bring a conflict between you and your employers."

"Oh, don't worry about that," Josie answered before Helen could speak. "Mama has been hinting around to Helen that you would make her a good husband." Josie ignored Helen's horrified gasp. "I know she will agree to let us visit you."

With a face she knew was flaming red, Helen watched North's expression to gauge his reaction. She was relieved when he appeared to be happy with that news.

Helen's gaze slowly lowered to Josie, and

she saw the young girl looking at her with a sheepish expression. "I'm in quite a lot of trouble, aren't I?" she whispered in an apologetic voice.

"You can be assured of it," Helen whispered back as they entered the main yard of the plantation.

Helen scanned the lawn and noticed for the second time just how many young women were in attendance. Most of them she'd never seen before this day.

And when the sound of the carriage drew everyone's attention, every single female smiled and began to walk straight for the barouche.

There was only one word running through Helen's mind, and it wasn't a nice one.

Competition!

CHAPTER 9

"Hello, Reverend Campbell!" said the one with the huge blue bonnet decorated with lighter blue flowers.

"Yoo-hoo! Over here, Reverend," said the brunette in the bright yellow dress.

"I truly enjoyed your sermon this morning," said the one with the light blond hair as she fluttered her eyelids.

What a liar! Helen thought mean-spiritedly, her mood darkening with each little shrill giggle. He had barely handed Josie and Helen down from the barouche before the ladies surrounded him, all giving North one simpering compliment after the other.

North looked a little dazed, as he appeared to be trying to make sense of their words, since they were talking all at once.

Helen and Josie were both wearing frowns as they watched him being led from them over to where the table of food was set.

"It's like watching a bunch of crabs all

trying to grab hold of a baited string at one time," Josie commented. Since Helen had no idea what she was talking about, she would have to take the younger girl's word for it.

"He's certainly not fighting off their attentions," she observed but then felt petty for voicing it aloud.

"I think he's just overwhelmed!"

"Hmm." Helen sounded skeptical as she continued to watch North. They were actually preparing him a plate of food, each one adding to it. They were creating a small mountain not even three men could possibly eat.

"Girls! You've lost him!" Imogene cried for their ears only as she came running hurriedly up to them. "Helen, you must do something!"

She had to be joking! "Mrs. Baumgartner, what can I possibly do? He doesn't seem to mind the attention," Helen told her, and again she heard the jealousy in her tone.

Imogene waved her hand as if to refute her words. "Of course he does." She sucked in a loud breath. "Did you see that?" she asked excitedly as she pointed in North's direction. "He's looking around. . . . See! He looks like he needs rescuing! So *go!*"

All Helen saw was North looking at the

pile of food on his plate with something akin to horror and then peering around for a place to sit. That was quickly resolved for him when the blue-bonnet girl led him to an empty table.

"I'm going to get something to eat," Helen said instead of responding to Imogene's urgings. Determinedly she began to walk toward the table of food.

"But, Helen!" Imogene pleaded after her. Still, Helen doggedly kept walking. It took a lot of willpower not to look at North when she passed his table, which was now occupied by all the ladies.

"Helen!" She thought she heard him call, but it could have only been her wishful thinking.

These women were ridiculous in their behavior, Helen observed as she heard them giggle and chatter. In England, never would a girl go up to a man she hadn't been introduced to and speak to him.

It was too bad North couldn't remember that!

Or maybe he did, she amended her thoughts, as she plopped the food on her plate without really paying attention to what she was getting.

She found a table on the other side of the

lawn from where North sat with his admirers.

When she realized she had scooped a large amount of collard greens onto her plate, a vegetable that was her least favorite food, she sighed and pushed her plate away. She really wasn't hungry anyway.

She was jealous, and it was silly to feel that way, really. Everyone believed North to be their clergyman and wanted to know him better. And since there was quite a shortage of young, marriageable men in the area, they probably all had higher hopes they could know him *much* better.

" 'It isn't ladylike to pout,' " Josie quoted, as she sat beside her while placing her plate of food on the table. Helen could tell Josie had managed to fill her plate without her mother looking on, for it was filled with slices of cake and pie. " 'It puts one's face in an unattractive position and causes tiny lines to form between one's eyes. . . .' " She paused from her speech, in which she used an exaggerated English accent, and thought a moment. "Or was the 'lines between the eyes' thing for when one is jealous *and* angry?"

Helen sighed. "I suppose I have become a bit fond of North." She nibbled on a piece of bread and then noticed the boiled crawfish on her plate. *How did that nasty little creature get there?* She could never understand how civilized people could get so much enjoyment out of cracking open the outer shells and biting the meat out of the tail with their teeth.

She knew ladies of London's society who would faint dead away at the sight of such a spectacle.

"I may be only thirteen, but I am not blind, Helen. I could tell you were in love with him the moment you realized who he was on that first day. Even Mother agrees."

She spoke like a woman of twenty! "You are too young to know what love is," Helen countered as she carefully picked up the crawfish by one of its pinchers and tossed it onto Josie's plate.

"Oh, thank you!" Josie automatically responded. And just as Helen knew she would, she cracked and peeled the shellfish in no time at all.

Helen shuddered.

"I do know about love." Josie picked up the conversation after she had wiped her hands on her cloth napkin. "My father left behind a title and his father's riches because he loved my mother. One day I'll find love like that." She sighed dreamily as she said this, and Helen didn't remind her of her earlier statement about not even liking boys.

Helen also didn't mention the fact that Josie's father wasn't exactly poor after he was disinherited, either. She wondered if he'd have married Imogene if there had been no inheritance from his mother and if they'd had to start from nothing. She looked across the lawn and saw Robert walk by his wife at that moment. Before continuing to where his friends were standing, he put a hand on her shoulder and squeezed it. A sweet gesture. Perhaps he would have married her no matter what.

"I hope you will find true love, Josie," Helen said instead as she finally allowed her gaze to settle on North. She was startled to see him staring straight at her. She glanced around him and noticed there were other people besides the young women around him now.

North smiled at her, then looked back to the man on his right, who appeared to be speaking to him.

Helen sighed dreamily, already forgetting her earlier jealousy. That smile from North had undone all the hurt she'd felt over being pushed out of the way by the other girls.

It was then she became aware that the blond girl with the fluttery eyes was still sitting next to him. North was looking at her, and she seemed to be telling him something.

Suddenly Helen was struck by a horrible thought. What if North fell in love with someone else? Not only would it make Helen terribly sad, but it could also spell disaster if North got his memory back!

If he fell in love with any of these young ladies and even married one of them, he could wake up one day and realize his whole life was a lie. He and his future wife would be devastated. It would be more disastrous than if he married Helen.

Steps had to be taken to ensure this did not happen!

She was going to have to embarrass herself. There was just no other way about it!

"I'll be right back!" she told Josie as she jumped up from her chair, then all but ran over to where North was sitting . . . still talking to *Blondie!*

What do I say? What do I do? she asked herself over and over as she drew nearer to him. It had to be some reasonable excuse to pull him away from his table and from *her!*

"Uh . . . Reverend . . . uh . . . Campbell!" she stuttered as she tried to catch her breath and remember what to call him. "I . . . uh . . ."

She drew a complete blank. She glanced about the table and noticed every eye was on her, curious as to what she was about to say.

"Uh . . ." Nothing. She wondered if this was how North felt this morning when he was trying to deliver his sermon. Her eyes strayed to the blond, and there was a certain smirk about her rosy lips that suggested she knew what Helen was up to.

"What's wrong, Miss Nichols?" North asked, his tone more questioning than concerned.

"Uh . . ." She stalled again. She glanced at the blond again and noticed she was back fluttering her eyes at North, trying to get his attention.

It was the eye-fluttering thing that inspired her.

She began to bat only one of her eyes. "My eye!" Batting one eye was not an easy thing to do. "I believe there is something in it."

North looked at her with a somewhat bemused expression. "It looked fine just a moment ago."

"It comes and goes," she answered quickly, realizing how ridiculous she sounded. But since she had begun the ruse, she might as well finish it. "Would you mind stepping over there in the sunlight and looking at it for me?" She pointed to a spot far from the shaded area they were seated in.

"Pardon me, but might I be of some help?" the man beside North questioned, finally bringing all the attention off Helen and onto him. "I am Dr. Giles. I have a practice in New Orleans, but I come through Golden Bay every month to check on everyone here. Why don't I take a look at it?"

"Oh . . ." Helen sounded like a deflating balloon. Just like her bright ideas! "I suppose that would be all right," she relented after coming up with no reasonable excuse to turn down his offer of help.

"I'll walk with you," North chimed in, and Helen could have kissed him. Did he know what she'd been up to? "I will hold your hand while the doctor performs the surgery," he added teasingly. One quick glance at his eyes told her she hadn't fooled him one bit.

"Never take the eyes lightly, Reverend," the doctor cautioned, unaware of Helen's subterfuge. "One tiny shard of wood or glass can cause a world of damage."

"Of course, Doctor," North answered contritely as they followed the older man, who was dressed rather more like the dandies of the English ton than the usual American mode of dress she'd seen thus far. His coat was a rich gold color with red trim at the sleeves and lapel. The vest underneath matched the ruby color of the trim and was made of shiny brocade. Considering every other man at the picnic wore more somber colors in shades of black, gray, and brown, he quite stood out.

Helen felt ridiculous as Dr. Giles examined her eye. He kept making the sound *mm-hmm,* and she wondered if he actually saw anything.

He didn't. "I'm afraid I cannot tell you the source of your irritation," he finally told her, looking perplexed.

Helen could have told him her source of irritation had blond hair and was flirting with the man she loved. Instead she thanked him for at least going to the trouble of examining her. "Perhaps the wind blew it out," she offered.

He accepted that it could have happened, and both she and North walked him back to the table.

Blondie was still there. Waiting. She was already smiling at him, and the fluttering eyelids would certainly be next! "Nor . . . uh . . . Reverend! Would you walk me back to my table? I just wanted to have a word with you for a minute."

North didn't even look surprised by her

request. "Of course. Will you excuse me?" he asked to the table at large, and Helen was glad to notice he didn't so much as glance at the blond.

"If you wanted to talk to me, Helen, there was no need to go to such theatrics. Next time, just ask," he told her in a low voice as he smiled at her, flashing his even, white teeth.

Helen's face felt heated with embarrassment. "I noticed the blond girl was so ill-manneredly monopolizing all your time, and so I thought that since you might not know how to extricate yourself without hurting her feelings, I tried to do it for you," she offered, the lengthy explanation hardly making sense even to her.

But North agreed. "Aye, I was feeling quite uncomfortable. I might not remember much, but I do know the young ladies here are not skilled in the art of ladylike manner or etiquette. These are some of the finest families in the area, and yet I do not understand why this facet of their children's upbringing is overlooked."

"Many of the English families are not former nobility such as Robert Baumgartner is but have come from little or nothing and become wealthy with hard work. I've heard the Creole plantations are a little different because more of them are from aristocratic families hailing from mostly France and Spain." Helen shrugged. "That is why I am here. The Baumgartners wanted to make sure their younger daughter was taught those things."

They both looked to see Josie still sitting at the table, stuffing cake into her mouth. Helen noticed there was white frosting smudged on both cheeks, and she, along with North, began to laugh. "Whether she will follow your teachings is quite another thing altogether."

Helen laughed more. "I'm afraid you are right. Even her sister was having a tough time adjusting to all the rules of society when last I saw her." Helen thought about the beautiful and friendly Claudia Baumgartner whom she'd met while visiting London with Christina. "Claudia is determined to be the lady that her grandfather, the Marquis of Moreland, wants her to be, yet I can't help feeling she's very unhappy. It's like seeing a caged tiger at a circus that you know just longs to be free."

"Did I ever meet her?" North asked, and Helen remembered that indeed she had seen him talking to her once.

"I believe you had been introduced," she answered truthfully, for she had no idea if he was better acquainted with her or not.

North and Helen sat down at the table, and Josie chose that moment to get up, announcing she was going for another round.

North laughed. "She is going to be sick."

"Not if Mrs. Baumgartner sees her!" Helen peered over her shoulder to where Josie had just reached the dessert table. Just as she knew she would, her mother was there to intercept and lead her over to the regular food.

They chatted for a moment, topics ranging all the way from the weather to the people they'd met in Golden Bay. Finally their words drifted away, and for a sweet moment, they sat looking into one another's eyes, neither looking away. Helen was surprised to have no feeling of awkwardness, and she got the impression he felt the same.

"Helen, if I may be so bold as to ask this, what is there between you and me?" he suddenly came out with, surprising them both. He sat back, rubbing a hand over his face. "I am sorry to have spoken so forcibly out of turn," he began to apologize.

"No, it is all right," Helen expressed, her heart pounding with fear and expectation all at one time. "You cannot remember anything, so —"

"But you see, it is not that reason for which I am speaking." He looked around as if to see if anyone had heard his impassioned statement, and then let out a breath. "I am experiencing feelings for you I feel did not just begin when I first saw you two weeks ago. It's as though my heart remembers even though my mind cannot. I know we did not act upon them, but was there a mutual attraction between us?"

Helen could only be confused by his words. North had never given her any indication he felt anything but friendship for her when they were in England. He thought her pretty — this much she knew from Christina — but wouldn't she have sensed anything deeper from him? When he looked at her with his dazzling, friendly smile, wouldn't she have read something more in the depths of his blue gaze?

She had certainly looked hard enough for any sign, any shred of love or deep affection.

She had lied to this man and misled him on so many things. And even though she had the golden opportunity to make him believe there was more between them so that he would feel more confident to pursue her, she just couldn't tell another lie.

"I will tell you honestly, North, that I

never knew you thought of me as anything but a friend. If you felt more, then I was not aware of it," she told him, careful not to mention her own feelings.

North shook his head. "I know I must have, Helen. The question is, why did I not act upon it? Why did I not call upon you and pursue what I know I must have been feeling in my heart?"

Helen tried to comprehend what he was telling her, but she couldn't believe it. Surely he had to be wrong! North had feelings for her when he knew he was a duke?

Helen thought back on the times she last saw him and realized that he started to avoid her at the balls she would attend. He would say no more than a few words before he'd excuse himself to go talk to a friend and such. Could it have been because he liked her more than he should yet saw no hope in it?

Helen looked at North, with his lock of golden hair falling in a wave over his brow and the stylish yet simply made suit, which was tight about his shoulders. His handsome looks and elegance did not fit the image everyone had put him in. They thought he was a clergyman, so they did not look past that title to grasp that this was no ordinary, common man.

"Perhaps your family would not have approved of me. I am, after all, just a gentleman farmer's daughter. They could have been pressuring you to settle on a woman of means," she offered truthfully.

"Hmm," North sounded, rubbing his chin thoughtfully. "I had not thought of that. It would seem like, judging from my attire, my family may have been in a financial quandary. Perhaps they were pressuring me to find an heiress," he murmured more to himself than to her, as if he were trying to reason it all out.

Abruptly he raised his head and smiled like a man who knew all the answers. "I have it all figured out!" he declared.

Helen felt as though her heart had fallen to the pit of her belly. "You remember everything?" she asked, trying not to sound dismayed by that prospect.

North, however, shook his head. "Unfortunately no, but I have been struck with insight! I know the reason I came to America!"

Helen blinked, trying to adjust to the path their conversation had taken. With North, she felt like she was often riding on a wild carriage ride, not knowing where they were heading or what sudden turns they might take. "It wasn't to be their preacher?" she offered, interested to know what scenario his mind had conjured up.

"Helen, I chose Louisiana because I knew you were going to be here!"

CHAPTER 10

One week then two passed, yet Helen could not stop thinking about North's words at the picnic. Though she tried to dissuade him from his reasoning, he would not be influenced. To him, everything made perfect sense, and he treated his "epiphany," as he called it, almost like it was a true memory.

Helen frankly did not know what to do or say when North wanted to talk about it. Which he did — quite a lot. He wanted to know about each meeting they had, what they said, and how they treated one another.

It was so taxing on her poor nerves that Helen began to make excuses to stay away from his house. But that didn't work because he would just come down to the plantation to see her. It was an easy thing to do since he had an ally in the house, namely Imogene Baumgartner.

One good thing that happened was that North's preaching, thanks to Josie and

Helen's helping him prepare, was greatly improved on the next Sunday, and one might say even inspiring on the third one. He seemed to be acclimating himself within the community as he visited families and prayed for their sick. As odd as it was, he seemed to be thriving in the occupation he was never meant to perform.

Helen would give herself headaches at night just thinking about the what-ifs. What if he never got his memory back? Would he be happy and content as Hamish Campbell? What if he didn't remember until he was fifty? Would he want to rush back to England and try to acclimate himself to his old life, or would he decide to continue as a preacher?

Helen was certainly no philosopher about life's mysteries, but it sure opened her mind to possibilities outside what she'd always known. She even raised the question to herself as to whether God had, indeed, meant for North to take poor Hamish Campbell's place.

But He didn't mean for you to lie and break one of His commandments, a voice would always remind her whenever she began to justify herself and her actions.

A knock sounded at her door, pulling Helen from her pondering. It was Monday morning, and she was supposed to have been brushing her hair but had, as usual, gotten lost in her thoughts.

After Helen called out for her visitor to come in, Imogene Baumgartner walked into the room, her face clearly upset. "Helen, I have just heard the most devastating news," she stated right away, her voice full of sorrow as she pulled a chair up so she could sit beside Helen.

Helen immediately thought of North. "Has something happened to Reverend Campbell?" she cried, not even realizing how easily his false name just rolled off her tongue.

Imogene quickly assured her that wasn't it. She placed her hand over Helen's and told her, "It concerns Lord Trevor Kent, the Duke of Northingshire, who is related to our friends at the Kent plantation."

Uh-oh, Helen thought with mounting dread. In the few weeks North had been in Golden Bay, not once had she considered that if North were here, everyone else in the world would presume he was dead. How incredibly selfish and single-minded she had been!

"I'm afraid he has been declared missing and assumed to be dead," Imogene said gently, speaking the words Helen had already assumed would be the news. "I believe Josie said you knew him?"

Helen glanced at her and then quickly lowered her eyes, hoping to give her employer the notion that she was shocked by the news. "Yes, but I knew him only as an acquaintance while I was in England," she said softly and carefully, trying not to lie yet not wanting Imogene to know of her feelings for the duke.

"Oh, then I am truly sorry," she offered in condolence as she patted Helen's hand again. "I have often heard from the Kents of what a fine man he'd been and how generous he was to his friends and loved ones. I had been hoping to meet him."

Helen listened to Imogene and heard her sigh sadly. "He was very nice to me when I first met him," Helen said, feeling like she needed to say something. In truth, she felt sick inside as she thought of his poor relatives and what they must be going through. Then she asked, trying to keep the worry from her voice, "Have they notified his family in England?"

She was relieved when Imogene shook her head. "No, they said they would search a little longer before they sent word. They are hoping against all odds that he still lives."

Helen wanted to cry. What was she to do

now? Again the situation had grown more complicated.

"Well, I'll leave you to your grooming," the older lady said, as she got up from her seat and straightened the bow on the high waist of her fawn-colored morning dress. She was almost at the door when she seemed to suddenly remember something. "Oh! I also wanted to ask a favor of you."

Helen, still overwhelmed by this latest obstacle, nodded absently.

"Pierre, poor dear, is sick this morning with what appears to be some sort of stomach ailment. Is there any way you and Josie could take the barouche and make sure Reverend Campbell has all he needs today? Pierre tells me he still burns everything he tries to cook, and I know you have some knowledge in this area . . . ?" She let her voice drift off in a question.

Helen managed to curve her lips into a smile that she truly did not feel. "Of course I'll go."

"Excellent! I normally would have one of the house servants go, but since I know you like to spend time with him, I didn't think you would mind," she told her in a gentle, teasing tone and then left the room.

Yes, Helen loved spending time with North; but the more she was in his presence, despite their growing feelings for one another, the more she got the feeling that a future between them could never be.

There was a great deal of self-pity in North's thoughts and even in his walk as he practically dragged himself from his little house out to the barn. He'd sat in his house an hour after he'd received word that Pierre wouldn't arrive, hoping someone would be sent as a replacement.

No one came.

So he came to terms with the fact that if he didn't go out and retrieve the milk and eggs himself, plus get a slab of bacon from the underground ceramic urns that served as a way to keep his food cool, he was going to starve.

Well, he amended to himself, he would certainly be very hungry. That would lead to his being cranky, and he would be unable to begin to study his new sermon for the upcoming Sunday.

Since he was actually beginning to enjoy his studies of the Bible and finding just the right message to share with his congregation, he decided to search for nourishment.

So here he was, about to enter his least favorite place in this world . . . his barn.

He had to admit he was getting better at

milking the cow, although he managed to connive Pierre into doing it most days.

Thankfully, this morning Queen Mary must have "been in the mood" because she gave over her milk without a lot of fuss. The chickens were another matter altogether, however. They seemed not at all like themselves; instead, they were restless, jittery, and unwilling to part with their eggs as usual.

He finally managed to grab a few but not without war wounds to show for his struggle.

He'd no sooner swung open his heavy barn door when he spotted the source of his chickens' anxieties. There, stretched out straight with his mouth wide open toward North, was the most ferocious, ugly beast he'd ever encountered.

Alligator!

What had he heard about them? His mind raced. Did they attack? Did they eat humans? The creature chose that moment to snap his jaws shut and crawl forward a couple of inches as if showing North what he was capable of.

North didn't doubt him one little bit!

The wise course of action at this moment, he knew, would be to get away from the alligator as quickly as possible. The problem was that when the reptile moved forward, he blocked the door from being shut, and there was no other door in the barn.

Except . . .

North glanced around to gauge the distance between himself and the ladder to the loft. From there he could try to jump out of the hayloft door.

Hopefully he would not break a leg and arm in the process!

As he turned and sprinted toward the ladder, he held tight to his bucket of milk and basket of eggs. Climbing was a lot more difficult with them, but there was no way he was letting that beast take what he'd worked so hard to get!

Once he was out of harm's way, North watched the alligator to see if it would go away.

It didn't.

For what seemed like hours but actually was only minutes, the creature just lay there, not moving one muscle, despite the fact that his animals were all restless and moving about noisily.

Even *they* recognized danger.

After a few more minutes, North concluded he was going to have to try to jump from the loft. For all he knew, it might be days before the creature would decide to leave.

It took him a moment to locate a rope to lower his items. He was in the process of tying them together when he heard a movement from below. Quickly North scrambled to the loft door leading to the outside and peered down.

He nearly toppled out of the small door when he spotted Sam cradling the now-dead alligator in his arms as he walked out of his barn.

"What are you doing here?" he barked brusquely. He suddenly felt ridiculous, hiding up in his hayloft while the Indian had taken no more than a few seconds to take care of the problem.

Sam didn't so much as glance up as he tied the reptile to the back of his horse. The black gelding stirred in protest because of the weight of his new passenger. "Rescuing you from an alligator, preacher man," he answered sardonically, as he checked then double-checked his knots.

North, feeling less than a man, backed away from the small door and, with his milk and eggs, made his way back down the ladder. He placed his goods down on a table and then walked out to meet Sam. North noticed him examining his small garden.

"I have something to put on the soil of these carrots that will help them grow," Sam offered. Again he hadn't even looked up to see North walking toward him, and North was sure he hadn't made a sound while walking on the soft grass.

"Thank you, but I have my own way of gardening," he answered, knowing it was childish but finding it hard not to show his irritation where the swaggering Indian was concerned.

North heard Sam make a snorting sound, which just made him more irate.

"How many gardens have you planted?" Sam asked, this time standing up and looking straight at North. The Indian had an unnerving stare.

North couldn't know for sure, but he was almost certain he'd never even *walked* around a vegetable garden in his entire life. "Is there a reason for this visit?"

Sam smirked at him, still giving him that odd stare. It made North, for the first time, wonder if he'd been a violent man in his past, because he truly wanted to hit him.

The truth was, however, that North felt strangely inferior to the Choctaw. He seemed to be a man of the earth, capable of defending, feeding, and protecting himself and anyone he cared about. He appeared comfortable with this wild, untamed land, whereas North constantly felt like an outsider.

North was smart enough to know he shouldn't compare himself to the Indian, because they were raised in two different worlds and taught very different things, but he found he did anyway.

He hated not being able to do simple things for himself. He even had trouble dressing himself and was almost certain he'd had a servant to do it for him in Scotland.

He didn't want to be pampered and waited on. He didn't want the kind of life he saw the plantation owners leading, where servants or slaves did everything for them and they did nothing for themselves.

"In your country, what do you do when another man wants the lady who you want?" Sam asked, bringing North's attention back to the smirk he was still sporting.

North had a feeling this was the reason why Sam had come. "The lady chooses the one she loves," he stated with confidence, knowing with all his heart that Helen was falling in love with him. It was in every glance, every smile she gave him. As far as he was concerned, Sam wasn't a rival for her affections.

Sam surprised him by bursting out with a loud, mocking sort of laugh — the kind that really set North's teeth on edge. "You let your women decide? Your people do things peculiarly!"

"And just how do *your people* do things?" North countered. "Throw the women over your horses and whisk them off to your caves until they relent?"

"Since we don't have caves in Louisiana," Sam began, his voice slow and deliberate as though he were talking to a child, "we issue a challenge to our opponent."

North didn't like the sound of that. With a disapproving frown, he told him, "Are we talking about a duel? Because I am most certain they are illegal."

Sam sighed and looked skyward as if trying to hold on to his patience. "This is another thing that irritates me with *your* people. You jump right away to the worst conclusion." He turned and walked back to his horse and withdrew a bow. "This is what I am talking about. A challenge. A contest to see who the better man is."

North eyed the bow and made every effort to pretend to be unfamiliar with one. He knew instinctively that he was familiar with how to handle the weapon. "You want to challenge me to an archery contest?"

North asked, to make sure he understood that they weren't going to be shooting arrows at each other. "And if I don't know how to handle a bow . . . ?"

Sam shrugged, his overconfident smirk back on his face. "There are always guns or knives."

North wanted so badly to accept the Indian's offer and show him that he was just as much of a man as Sam was. But he had the distinct feeling Helen would not be pleased, and neither would his congregation, once they found out their preacher was in a contest to win a girl's affections!

"Well, Sam, as interesting as that sounds, I will have to turn your offer of challenge down," he told him and watched the Indian's face turn to disappointment.

North couldn't help but wonder if the Indian was trying to befriend him in his own odd little way. "But I would love to join you for target practice sometime. Maybe even try my hand at hunting," North impulsively offered, just to see if he would accept.

Sam appeared interested but only after he studied North a moment, unsure of the preacher's motives. "I will come by in two days," he told him and then pointed toward the alligator. "I'll bring you half of the meat I get from the alligator tail, too."

Alligator tail? North didn't say a word. He didn't want Sam thinking he was less of a man because he'd never eaten any. He'd eat every bite if it killed him!

Sam gathered the horse's reins and began to walk off when he unexpectedly stopped and turned for one last comment. "I am still determined to marry Helen Nichols, preacher man," he stated, wanting that particular point understood.

"So am I," North countered, knowing he truly did want nothing more than to marry Helen.

They exchanged a measuring look, and then without another word, Sam grinned and turned to walk away.

Both were surprised to see Helen come from around the house with Josie. "Sam!" she exclaimed, clearly shocked to see him. "What are you doing here?"

"Alligator hunting" was all Sam said as he walked past her, tugging his horse behind him.

Helen opened her mouth as if to say something as she turned to watch him walk away, but no words seemed to come out.

"Did you really go alligator hunting, Reverend North?" Josie asked, using her own version of his name, as she ran up to him, her long, bound hair bouncing as she went.

North reached out and gave her hair a playful yank that made her giggle. There was absolutely no way he was going to tell them what really happened. A man had to maintain some sort of dignity. "Something like that."

"You weren't fighting with him, were you?" Helen asked as she, too, walked up to meet him. "Sam can be a little overbearing, but I wouldn't let him aggravate you. He lives by a whole different set of rules than any other man I know."

North reached out and pulled a ladybug off Helen's shoulder. It was interesting to note that she didn't flinch or jerk away from his touch. Instead she looked at his hand and smiled as the red bug flew away. "Sam *is* very different from most white men," he noted, watching to see what her reaction would be to his next words. "Some women like the outdoorsy, rough-and-tough type that he is."

He almost laughed when Helen actually shuddered. "I don't know of any woman who enjoys polite society and gently bred manners who would want Sam as a husband!" she stated emphatically.

"I would!" Josie piped up, causing both of

the adults to gape at her with astonishment. "He wouldn't care if I had any manners at all!"

Helen shook her head disapprovingly. "You will not get out of learning your lessons on the art of curtsying today, so stop trying."

Josie made a *humph* sound and folded her arms defiantly at her chest. "Why do I need to learn that? I'm an American! We don't bow down to anyone!"

North exchanged a long-suffering glance with Helen; then she looked back down and answered, "Your sister will one day be the Marchioness of Moreland. She will have to bow before the king, and you and your parents will have to do the same thing."

Josie rolled her eyes and made a growling noise. "I'm going to talk to the chickens. At least there I don't have to be polite or remember my manners."

Helen and North laughed softly as the young girl stomped into the barn.

"You know, if Sam can wait a bit, Josie just might be the perfect match for him," North observed. "But you can't always choose the person you fall in love with. And if he is truly in love with you, he might not want anyone else."

North saw a sadness fall over Helen's face

as she murmured wistfully, "That's true."

He bent his head toward her and brought her chin up so she was looking directly into his eyes. "Helen," he began, almost afraid to ask the question. "Were you once in love with someone?"

She just stared at him for a moment, and North wasn't altogether sure she was going to answer him. But finally she did, and the answer hit him squarely in the heart. "Yes, once. A few years ago."

His hand was still on her chin, and she didn't seem to mind when his thumb began to softly caress the skin along her jawline. "What happened?"

"Nothing. He was not a man of my station. In fact, he was way above it." She paused as if she were gauging his reaction. "He was a nobleman, and though we were friends, he chose not to pursue a relationship outside of that friendship."

A fire lit within North's heart, and indignation for her hurt flowed from his lips. "That is preposterous!" he articulated passionately. "To throw away a chance at love that may only come once in one's lifetime, just because of one's birth, is an injustice to God and all He created us to be."

He spoke it with such fervor and with such vehemence that North had the feeling he'd grappled with this very situation before; only it had been he who'd faced such a decision.

He realized then that Helen was looking at him as if she didn't believe a word he said.

CHAPTER 11

Helen could only stare at North with marked disbelief as he moved his hand from her chin to run it through his hair in a gesture of perplexity. It wasn't so much what he said but *how* he said it. It was like someone trying to make a case for himself.

What *did* that mean? Did he once grapple with the same feelings — go through the same situation?

Helen could barely think it, although she couldn't help but hope for it.

Had he been in love with her after all?

But another thought followed directly after that one — if he *had* been in love, he hadn't acted on his feelings. In fact, he'd even started seeking her out less and less at gatherings.

What did *that* mean?

Finally she voiced part of her musings. "You speak as though you have struggled with this dilemma yourself. Did you remember something?"

She held her breath until she saw him shake his head no. "It's odd, really. I feel as though I've made the same argument before, but where? Had you once told me this? Is that what I'm remembering?"

Helen shook her head. "No, I've never told anyone except my best friend, Christina." And she had always tried to discourage Helen from letting her attraction to North grow, for she feared Helen would be hurt.

North looked so confused and seemed to be trying hard to remember something that would make sense to him. It compelled Helen to reach out spontaneously to hold his hand. The gesture seemed to freeze North for a moment, as his eyes focused on their hands.

Uh-oh. She was being too familiar. Too forward. "I'm sorry, I didn't mean . . . ," she began to ramble as she tried to pull her hand away, but he held fast and interrupted her.

"No! Please . . . ," he cried softly as he looked directly into her eyes, his own searching as if trying to decipher her thoughts. "I like it that you feel so comfortable with me."

She smiled shyly, aware of the change of

mood between them — of how important this particular moment seemed to be. Her feelings were so overwhelming to her that she had to remind herself even to breathe.

"I just need to ask you one thing," he said softly, pulling her closer to him. "Are you still in love with the nobleman?"

Now that is a tricky question, Helen thought, panicking for a brief instant. But as she thought of the man she knew in England versus the man she knew him to be here in America, she knew she could answer truthfully. "No, my feelings are not what they were."

North emitted a breath of relief as he looked down for a moment and took her other hand, bringing both of them to his lips. "Helen, you must know of the growing feelings I have for you." She nodded jerkily, still having a hard time comprehending she was standing so close to North. "I would like to openly begin calling on you," he explained. "That would mean everyone would know you and I have an affection for one another, and that includes the congregation. You might come under some scrutiny, so I wanted to warn you beforeha—"

Helen stopped him by putting her fingers over his lips. "Yes," she gushed excitedly, unable to contain her joy.

He took hold of her hand again. "Are you sure?"

She nodded, and they stared into one another's eyes again. Helen forgot that almost everything about their relationship was built on a lie. She forgot the guilt she'd been under and the fear of what might happen in the future. For this one moment, she was going to revel in the love she had carried for so long for this man and remember it when she was old and alone with nothing but memories to get her through.

North leaned forward to brush a stray hair that had blown across her cheek, and when Helen turned to see what he was doing, they found themselves nose to nose.

North paused and looked at her searchingly. And whatever he'd been looking for, he must have found, for he gently pressed a kiss to her lips.

Helen held tight to his hand as his mouth gently caressed hers. Her heart was beating madly, and her mind was swirling, trying to reconcile her old emotions with the brand-new feelings she was experiencing. All the romance and gothic books she had ever read had not even been close to describing the feeling of being in his arms and being kissed by him.

Perhaps God felt sorry for her a little bit,

and since He knew she would probably never live down the scandal of what she'd done to North and therefore never find a man who would want to marry her, He was giving her this little bit of bliss to live the rest of her life on.

Helen almost protested when he finally drew his head back and smiled at her. But the wonder in his eyes filled her heart with gladness as he gazed at her one last time before stepping away.

Helen suspected that North must have kissed a half-dozen or more women in his lifetime. But he didn't remember any of them, and kissing her was like his first time.

"I can't wait to tell Mama you kissed him!" Josie exclaimed, causing them to jump farther apart and guiltily look at the young girl.

Helen swallowed and threw North a nervous glance. "Uh, Josie, it might not be a good idea to tell your mother about this."

Josie frowned. "Oh, why not? I have to tell somebody!" She smiled, apparently coming up with a better idea. "I know! I'll tell Sam!"

"No!" Both Helen and North yelled out to her at the same time.

"You don't want to hurt his feelings, do you?" Helen tried to reason in a softer tone.

"Well, what good is it for me to know if I

can't brag about knowing something that no one else knows?"

Helen sighed, rubbing her temples, wondering if the child could ever be tamed. "Josie, later we shall discuss the merits of guarding our tongues."

"Why don't the two of you get the milk and eggs from the barn, and I'll get the bacon from the urns," North suggested, as he must have known Helen was growing weary of dealing with the young girl.

He knew her so well. "Yes, let's do that!" she agreed, eager to take everyone's mind off the kiss they had just shared.

Well, maybe not everyone should forget. Helen certainly could never forget it, and she had a feeling North wouldn't, either. Now if only Josie *would!*

The two of them took North's food into the kitchen, and she began to prepare the skillet over the fire. A knock sounded at the door.

Josie ran to open it. "Hi, Mrs. Chauvin!" she greeted, and Helen could hear a female voice telling her something from outside.

Helen got up and walked to the door to find Marie Chauvin standing there, holding what looked to be a letter.

"Oh! Hello, Helen," Marie greeted, surprised at finding Helen in the preacher's house. "Is the reverend here?"

Helen wondered what Marie was thinking. The middle-aged French woman, who was petite in stature and a little plump, was the wife of the area blacksmith and one of the nicest ladies Helen had met in the area. She was the perfect person to handle everyone's mail because she was not a gossip or nosey by any means. She knew the woman would not draw false conclusions and think the worst. However, Helen wanted to make it clear why she was here at North's house.

"He is around back, I believe. Josie and I were sent by Mrs. Baumgartner to make sure Reverend Campbell had breakfast. Pierre is sick and unable to help him today."

Marie smiled at the explanation, seeming to accept it at face value. "Ah yes. I know my husband would not be able to do one thing for himself if I were not there to do it for him. He'd probably starve."

Helen chuckled. "It was the same with my father," she told her. She looked down at the paper Marie was holding. "Did you need to tell him something? I know that he should be back any minute."

Marie smiled and waved the note in front of her face. "No, no. I'll just leave this with you, and you can pass it on to the reverend. I believe it's a letter from his sister, judging by the name and the postmark from Scotland. I remember my husband telling me he'd mentioned living with his sister in some of the correspondence we had with him."

It took everything in Helen to hide the dismay she was feeling as she reached out and took the letter.

She and Marie exchanged a little more small talk, which she could barely remember later; then Marie left.

For a moment she found herself just staring down at the letter with the scratchy penmanship addressed to Hamish Campbell. She couldn't help but feel sorrow for his sister and the fact that somehow she had to be told her brother was missing or most probably dead.

But how could Helen do that without North trying to write her back?

The web of deceit and the problems it was causing were growing thicker and more intricate every single day. When she got one thing under control, something else would pop up that made the situation worse.

"How come he never mentions his sister?" Josie asked. Helen could tell she was dying to read it.

So was Helen.

"Perhaps it makes him sad to talk about

her since she is so far away," Helen prevaricated. She noticed how easily false excuses just rolled off her tongue.

That definitely wasn't a talent to be proud of.

She then realized she had to give the letter to North when they were alone so he didn't make a slip and say he didn't know he had a sister or something equally as telling. Helen truly wished she could just hide the letter from him and write one back to the woman, giving her the bad news.

But Marie might ask him about receiving it. Then Helen would be in even more trouble.

What a calamity!

"Josie, would you see to the fire while I go and show this to North?"

In typical fashion, Josie made a face of protest but did as she was asked. The younger girl was obedient for the most part, even though she was extremely vocal about her opinions.

North was just coming up the side steps of the porch when Helen met him. He smiled at her in a way that let Helen know he was still thinking about their kiss and the new commitment they'd made to one another.

It was such a thrilling feeling to know he

liked her so much.

It was just too bad their relationship was built on nothing but deceit.

"North, Marie Chauvin came by to give you this. I wanted to make sure Josie wasn't around so you wouldn't be surprised to know that it is probably from your sister."

North looked at the letter she was holding out without even trying to take it from her. In fact, he looked at it as if he didn't want to open it at all.

His eyes flew back to hers, questioning. "I have a sister?"

Helen scrambled to find the right thing to say. "I didn't know," she explained, going with the truth. "I've never heard you mention a sister."

North looked back down at the letter, a frown of concentration on his face as he was trying to remember something . . . anything!

Slowly he reached out and took it from her. He read the name *Fiona Campbell* written above the seal. For a moment he seemed as though he wasn't going to open it.

Finally he lifted the seal and quickly read through the brief letter. "It is from my sister," he told her, his eyes still focused on the paper. "She writes that all is well in Melrose and for me not to worry about her. She says she has recently been called upon by a local sheep farmer whom she knows I would approve of." North looked up at Helen with troubled eyes. "She urges me to write back as soon as possible, Helen, but how can I when I can't even remember her?"

Helen's heart broke at the misery pouring from his voice and the despair in his eyes. Reaching out, she put her hand on his arm in a comforting gesture. "I will help you write it. There is no reason to tell her you've lost your memory. Just tell her about your church and the people living here."

He smiled at her and placed his hand atop hers. "I will tell her about you, too," he said low and tender.

Helen thought that was the sweetest thing she'd ever been told. Unfortunately she would have to find a way to make sure any letter that was written would never make it to Fiona Campbell's door.

She smiled at him, trying not to show how unsettled she was by this latest problem in her life. "Why don't I come by tomorrow and help you write it?"

He grinned broadly at her. "Why not today? Or are you just trying to come up with an excuse to see me tomorrow, also?" He tucked her hand in his arm and began to lead her to the door.

Actually she needed time to come up with

a plan. She did, however, like being with him any time she could. "I don't think I'll answer that, for I fear you are becoming too sure of yourself!"

North laughed as he opened the door and allowed her to enter first. "Ah! So that is the reason for the delay!"

She pretended to sniff at his comment as she stuck her chin up and looked down her nose at him. "Nonsense! Josie and I have lessons to finish, that is all."

"Ugh!" Josie sounded with more than a little disgust. "She never forgets!" she exclaimed with marked disbelief as she set the skillet down noisily on the metal rack of the fireplace.

Helen exchanged a look with North, and her heart skipped a beat when he teasingly winked at her. "Perhaps tomorrow I can talk her into a picnic that would take up most of the afternoon and therefore most of your lesson time," North suggested to Josie but kept his gaze on Helen.

Helen pretended not to like that idea. "I don't know. . . ."

"Oh, please say yes, Helen. A picnic sounds like such fun!" Josie pleaded, practically jumping up and down with excitement.

Helen thought a moment and then smiled

at Josie. "I know! I can teach you how a lady makes polite conversation during a picnic or some other sort of gathering. I have so many —"

"Do you see what I mean, Reverend? She never lets me take a day off from my studies!"

North bent down to Josie and whispered in her ear, though it was plenty loud enough for Helen to hear. "Perhaps I can distract her tomorrow so you can play or go fishing."

He straightened and looked back at Helen. She hadn't even realized how much time passed as they stared into one another's eyes until Josie pulled on North's coat and motioned with her finger for him to bend down to her.

With an equally loud whisper, she told him, "If you could just keep staring at her like that for a few more hours, I might be able to miss today's lessons, too!"

North laughed, and Helen felt her face heat up with embarrassment. With determination, she grabbed the basket of eggs and made her way to the skillet, ignoring North when he asked her if she knew what she was doing.

CHAPTER 12

The next morning, North woke to the wonderful smell of bacon frying and the sound of a French song being badly sung, bringing him to the conclusion that Pierre was in his house.

"Good morning, monsieur!" The smiling black man greeted North as he walked into the room. Pierre had just placed the freshly fried eggs on the table.

"Good morning, Pierre," he greeted as he looked at his friend carefully. "Are you quite sure you are well enough to be here?"

"Of course," he assured him. He set a glass of milk beside North's plate. "It was only one of those maladies that lasts about three-fourths of the day. By the time the sun had started setting, I was feeling better."

"Well, I said many prayers for you, and I'm ashamed to say some of them were very selfish ones on my part," he admitted honestly with a sheepish grin. "I hate to admit it, but I am not a man who is used to taking care of himself."

Pierre sat across from him and sipped on a cup of coffee, a beverage he was often fond of drinking. "You are not telling me anything I do not know, monsieur."

North frowned. "Am I so obviously inept?"

Pierre held up his hand and shook his head. "No, no, monsieur!" he assured. "But I see what no one else sees since I am here all day." He seemed to study him through the coffee's steam. "You seek to change, monsieur?"

North leaned forward, eager to talk to someone about what he'd been thinking over. "I do, Pierre. I suppose I've had things done for me all my life, and now that I'm here" — he threw his arms wide — "I see men who are well respected who do things for themselves. They are not waited on hand and foot!" he finished in an impassioned voice. He was discomfited to realize his voice had risen, and he was practically shouting.

But it didn't seem to faze Pierre. "If you are determined to change, then you can change, but it will take dedication," he stated firmly. "The important matter here is that you show a desire. Most men are satisfied to stay where they are and settle for what life has brought them."

Pierre was truly an amazing person. If all men were as passionate about what they believed and what they wanted out of life as he was, the world would be a greater place to live. Every day he and North talked about everything from the war to slavery and politics and even debated the merits of Cajun French cuisine versus true French. Pierre had an opinion for everything and profound insights about things North was sure he'd never even thought about.

They even discussed God and the Bible, and even then, he loved to hear Pierre's convictions about certain matters and how he was so careful to live his life the way he felt God was leading him, taking advantage of every open door.

That was the way North so wanted to be. He wanted to be a man God could look down upon and say, "He is a man after My own heart!"

The two of them chatted a bit more, and then Pierre remembered something. "Oh yes! I forgot to tell you I received good news yesterday. My sister, who lives in New Orleans, had a fine baby boy. It is her first boy after giving birth to four girls, so everyone is happy about the *le petit garçon*," he told North proudly and went on to tell what else his sister had written in a letter. North barely heard him.

A baby. North suddenly had a flash of a genuine memory of holding a baby. Afraid to even move lest he do something to make the memory disappear, North slowly closed his eyes and concentrated on what he was seeing in his mind.

He was in a garden filled with brightly colored flowers, and he was dressed in a very fine navy suit. A baby in a linen dressing gown was in his hands, and he was holding the infant up, talking nonsense to him, causing the dark-headed child to laugh.

He wasn't alone in the garden! With him were a man and two ladies. The man with dark brown curly hair was chatting with a lovely redhead. He knew instinctively they were in love with one another.

Suddenly the other woman, a beauty with wisps of black curls falling about her rosy cheeks, sat beside him. He looked over to her and felt a tugging at his heart like it always did whenever she was around. She reached for the baby, and he gave him to her. He watched her lovingly kiss the infant on the head.

"North?" She looked up at him, and he

noticed it was his Helen.

"Monsieur Campbell?" Pierre called out again, causing the memory to suddenly come to an abrupt halt. "Sir, are you all —"

"Wait a moment, Pierre," he said urgently as he put his fingers at his temples and tried desperately to bring the memory back.

"If you are ill with a headache, I . . . ," the servant tried again, but North interrupted with a shake of his head.

"No, no, it's not that," he said, sounding defeated. He knew the memory was lost for the time being. "I was remembering. . . ." He stopped when he realized what he was about to confess, then quickly thought of something else to say. "I was remembering something I told Helen," he said instead. He got up quickly from the table, not even noticing he'd barely touched his breakfast.

"Where are you going?" Pierre asked, also getting to his feet.

"Pierre, I'm sorry, but I need to ride over to the Golden Bay plantation. There is something I need to ask Helen about," he called out as he ran to his room to find his coat. He knew he wasn't making any sense, but he couldn't explain, either.

He dashed back out and found Pierre just leaning against the table, watching him — and looking at North as if he'd lost all his

181

senses. "You have to go . . . right *now?*"

North smiled apologetically as he glanced at the table and saw his uneaten meal. "I'm sorry, but it's important."

"You're not asking her to marry you, are you?" he asked suddenly, his voice wary.

North opened the door and turned to grin at his friend. "Not today," he answered mischievously. "Oh! Is there any way you can prepare a food basket for three? I've invited Helen and Josie for a picnic today."

Pierre barely got a nod in before North was out the door and running to the buggy in which Pierre drove over every day. He'd been told he could use it anytime he needed.

He was so eager to see Helen and ask her about his memory that the usually short trip seemed to take longer. It did, however, give him time to dwell on the images for a bit longer, to study them and try to figure out what he saw and how he felt. The main question that burned in his mind was the obvious one. It was the one thing he wanted to know before he asked anything else about Helen being in his memory.

Whose baby was he holding?

Finally when he had arrived, North jumped from the buggy and threw the reins to the stable boy who had come running up to meet him.

Luckily Mr. and Mrs. Baumgartner were either out of the house or busy with other things, so he was able to instruct the servant to fetch Helen right away for him without having to make small talk with her employers.

He was pacing back and forth in the library when she breezed into the room, her expression indicating her surprise. "North! What are you doing here so early?" He swung around to see her and noticed her hair was totally unbound and flowing around her face and shoulders. She had always had at least the sides of it pulled back before, so it fairly took his breath away to see it in its natural state.

"Your hair . . . ," he murmured, feeling a little dazed and momentarily forgetting what he'd come for.

Immediately her hands flew up to her head, and she began pulling it back. "Oh no! I ran out of the room so fast I forgot about my hair!"

"No!" he cried, putting out his hand to stop her. "It's . . . it's fine, I assure you."

She gave him a look that said she didn't really believe him, but she decided to let it drop. "Well," she said, as if not really knowing what else to say. "Would you like to sit down?" She motioned toward cushioned chairs that faced one another.

North spied a sofa on the other side of the room that was more to his liking. "How about there? We have a view of the window."

They both walked over to it and sat close together. North turned slightly askew so he could better see her, then took one of her hands. "Helen, I remembered something this morning, and I need to ask you about it."

North felt Helen stiffen at his words, and he assumed it was due to the excitement that he could actually be getting his memory back.

"Oh?" she said, and North got the feeling she was a little nervous about what he was going to say.

Helen had never been more nervous in her entire life. What had he remembered? How *much* had he remembered?

"Did you remember . . . everything?" she asked carefully

She was a little relieved when he shook his head. "No, actually it was only a small segment, but it really brought a lot of questions to my mind."

Helen swallowed, knowing this was not going to be easy. "All right. Suppose you tell me about it."

North explained what he'd seen of the three people being there and the baby. Helen knew exactly what he was talking about.

"First, I guess my biggest question is, whose baby was I holding? I think I was calling him Ty?" He shook his head as if the details were a little sketchy.

Helen nodded, feeling safe to answer that one. "Yes, that was Tyler Douglas Thornton, Nicholas and Christina's nephew. They were raising him for a while when everyone had thought Nicholas's brother had been lost at sea," she explained, hoping she wasn't giving him too much information.

But North only nodded thoughtfully and looked a little relieved. "I'll admit the baby had me worried. I'd wondered if you'd been married before and had a child or if I had. But then, of course, that is silly. You would have told me anything important such as that," he stated assuredly.

If he only knew what I've been keeping from him, she thought shamefully.

"I was friends with Nicholas, wasn't I?" he asked, as he seemed to be figuring things out.

"You were best friends," she affirmed. "Are you remembering anything else about him?"

185

He shook his head. "No, but when I think about him, I feel a strong bond between us." He smiled. "And I think you can guess who else I saw in that memory."

Helen could still remember the day like it was yesterday. It was probably the second time she'd ever talked to North, and she'd been so excited. "You saw me," she said with a wistful smile.

North rested his arm along the top of the sofa and touched the back of his hand to her smooth cheek. "I saw you," he confirmed, his voice husky with emotion. "I remember what I felt, too, when I looked at you. You had taken the baby from me and were holding him in your arms, and it made something in my heart yearn for things I'd never really thought of before."

Helen could hardly believe what she was hearing. This was a memory from North the nobleman, not North the commoner. "What was that?" she asked breathlessly, so anxious for his answer.

His hand reached back to cup behind her ear, sending goose bumps down her spine. "I wanted a family. A wife, a child." He frowned, as he appeared to be analyzing his memory again. "You know, it's so strange. There are so many pieces missing, but I'll just tell you what I remember feeling." He took a breath. "I remember looking at you and feeling such a strong attraction, but coupled with that was a sort of regret or . . . or maybe it was indecision. I just don't know. But it was like I had feelings that I believed could not be realized or shared."

"You've spoken of this before," Helen broke in, unable to stop herself as she remembered an earlier conversation.

"I know! But this time I felt it even stronger than before," he stressed, seeming so desperate for answers. "Why did I feel this way? I know we've been over this, but what was keeping me from pursuing a relationship with you?"

Tears began to sting the backs of Helen's eyes, and she quickly looked down so that he wouldn't see them. This was the frustration she had always felt when she was in his presence, and, too, here was the answer she'd always looked for.

And maybe she knew it deep inside all along.

He had wanted her but was not willing to defy society to have her.

"I can't tell you that," she answered finally as she looked up at him. The sudden anger she felt over his inability to take a chance had dried up all her tears. "I had no idea you felt that way, North. You never, ever let me believe you wanted anything more than friendship."

He turned more so he was almost fully facing her. Cupping both hands on either side of her face, he asked urgently, "What was the obstacle? Was it my family? Was it because I knew you loved someone else?"

Tears came to the surface again, and this time she could do nothing but let them fall. "I can't tell you that. Only you can know the answer," she said softly, her voice small and broken.

He stared deeply and intensely into her eyes, and she noticed his own seemed a little misty. "I don't know what it was," he said, his voice husky with emotion that she'd never heard before. "However, I will promise you this. When my memory returns and I find out what the barrier was that kept me away from you, I vow to you now that I will never let it come between us again."

Guilt and shame ate at her soul as she tried to shake her head, yet he held fast to her. "You can't make that promise," she cried, trying to speak sense to him. "Perhaps it was insurmountable."

She nearly started crying again when he smiled at her with wonder and love shining so brightly in his eyes. "Helen, I promise," he stated emphatically. Then as if to seal his word, he pressed his lips to hers in a solid, strong kiss that lasted only a few seconds but spoke more than words could ever say.

North reached into his coat pocket and produced a white handkerchief, and he proceeded to gently wipe the remaining wetness from her cheeks. "You're even beautiful when you cry," he teased.

"No, I'm not," she said, then sniffed and tried to look down.

North took her chin and brought her face back up. He appeared to study her skin carefully. "Well, there is the matter of the red nose." He nodded in mock seriousness. "Yes, the red nose definitely brings the compliment from beautiful down to merely lovely."

She laughed and slapped his hand away. "You're horrid," she laughingly charged.

He laughed and tucked his handkerchief back into his pocket. "Why don't we get a little fresh air while the temperature is still cool outside?"

Helen nodded, eager to take her mind off North's troubling vow. "I'll dart upstairs and get my shawl."

North followed Helen out of the room and watched her as she disappeared up the staircase.

He leaned on the railing, daydreaming about the poignant moment they'd just shared when a stern voice spoke behind him.

"That was quite a display back there," Imogene Baumgartner said crisply. North turned to see her looking every bit an irate guardian, with her lips stretched in a thin line and her blazing eyes narrowed on him with more than a little distrust.

"I beg your pardon?" he asked, although he knew she had seen the kiss. But had she heard what they'd said?

"Let's not play games, Hamish." He noticed she'd dropped the "Reverend." Not a good indication. "I saw you kissing her, and as I am Helen's guardian, I have a right to demand what your intentions are toward her."

Well, that was an easy question. "I love Helen and intend to marry her."

That took the wind right out of Imogene's sails. "Oh," she said, sounding quite deflated.

North stepped closer to her, his face set in a sincere, heartfelt expression. "Mrs. Baumgartner, what you saw in there was me reassuring Helen that my feelings for her are real and my intentions are true. I do intend to court her in a proper fashion before I ask for her hand, but there is no doubt in my mind Helen Nichols will become my wife."

Imogene just stared at him unblinkingly for a moment with her hand at her throat. Suddenly tears were pouring from her eyes. "I haven't heard such a romantic speech since Robert proposed to me even though he knew his father would disown him!" she blubbered. "I knew . . . I just knew you were the right man for our Helen!" She was crying so much that North felt compelled to reach back into his pocket and bring out his slightly soiled handkerchief again.

He gave it a wary examination, shrugged his shoulders, and handed it over to her.

Imogene never noticed.

CHAPTER 13

Helen, North, and Josie spent most of the morning down by the pier. After a spirited lesson in archery, which Josie was already pretty adept at, thanks to Sam, North sent for the basket of food from his house so they could have their picnic by the water.

"This chicken is delicious!" Josie said enthusiastically as she bit into a chicken leg, not caring that the juice was running down her chin.

Helen had a brief, uneasy moment while she wondered which one of North's chickens they were actually eating, but it truly was so delicious that she soon forgot to worry about it.

She did chide Josie for her unseemly manners. "Josie, please use your napkin. You are about to stain that dress, and you know how Millie fusses," Helen warned.

Hearing Millie's name mentioned did what Helen hoped it would do. Josie immediately wiped her mouth and started being more careful with her food.

North exchanged a smile with her, and though they'd exchanged pleasantries and small talk, she could tell he very much wanted to ask her more questions about his memory. It was difficult to do so with Josie around, however.

Finally he seemed to think of something he could ask in Josie's presence. "Oh yes! I meant to tell you I started the letter to my sister last night."

Helen took a sip of water and hoped she didn't look as though she were dreading the topic at hand. "You did? What did you say?"

North leaned down on the blanket, propping himself up with his elbow. "I confess I didn't get very far into it. I still need your help with it."

"Please tell me about your sister!" Josie insisted with interest. Helen knew that the girl missed her own sister dreadfully. "What is she like? Is she younger or older?"

Helen didn't have a clue, so she was powerless to help him. She watched as a glimpse of panic flashed on his face but was quickly masked. "Uh, let's see. . . ." He stalled as he threw a pleading look to Helen. "She is younger. Yes, I have a younger sister," he stated as if he were trying to convince himself. "And . . . she's nice! Really and truly nice."

Josie looked at him with a scowl, clearly not pleased with the lack of details. "Well, what else? What does she like to do for hobbies or entertainment?"

North thought again and suddenly smiled. "She likes to knit! She is knitting me a sweater and plans to send it to me as soon as she finishes it."

"Oh," Josie responded with lackluster. Abruptly she brightened and asked another question. "Does she like puppies?" Helen knew exactly where this line of questioning was heading. Josie's friend Sarah had received a puppy for her birthday, and now Josie wanted one, too.

Imogene was scared to death of anything with four legs, except maybe a horse.

"Uh . . ." North hedged. "I suppose so." When Josie turned her head to grab another plum from the basket, North mouthed *"Help me"* to Helen.

What was she supposed to do? She didn't know the woman, either!

"Josie!" Helen exclaimed quickly, as she saw the younger girl's mouth open, ready to ask another question. "Didn't you want to go fishing today? I believe Joseph said he would take you out in the pirogue."

Those were the magic words. Josie loved nothing better than to paddle down the bayou in the small boat where she might get to see an alligator or snake. "He did?" she gushed as she jumped up, throwing crumbs all over them. "I'm going to go pull on some britches!"

Helen knew she should say something about dressing like a boy, but she decided to let it be. Being able to talk to North alone was more important than what the little girl wore. "Just don't let your mother see you dressed that way."

"I'll sneak out the back way," she yelled over her shoulder as she raced to the house.

"I hate to disillusion you, but it's not going to be easy to turn her into a lady. I wouldn't be surprised if she deliberately sought to marry an Indian or even a more common man to avoid any sort of etiquette altogether," North commented as they watched Josie disappear from sight. He sat up and began to put the uneaten food back into the large wicker basket.

Helen sighed and reluctantly agreed. "She's already threatened it, but I just keep hoping something will change her mind."

North chuckled. "Like what? Holding out for a miracle, are we?"

Helen shook her head and with a secret

smile answered, "No, just a man." North raised his brows in question, and she explained, "All it will take, once she's a little older, is for a young man to totally captivate her. She'll strive to do everything she can, including remembering all the proper behaviors that I have taught her, just to show him she's worthy of his attentions."

North just stared at her as if he'd never heard of such a thing. "Is that what you did? When you wanted to attract the nobleman you've spoken of?"

Oh, dear! She hadn't meant for the conversation to take this turn. "I've always wanted to better myself," she replied truthfully. Christina was forever teasing about how Helen loved to know about the aristocracy — how they dressed and the way they conducted themselves and spoke.

It was ironic that for all those years she'd wished to marry a nobleman so she could live in the society she so admired, and she now wished North would remain a simple country preacher so they could continue to live their lives uncomplicated by titles and riches.

A disturbed look fell across North's face as he looked back down at the basket and started moving things around. "You will not be 'bettering yourself' if we marry," he said gruffly. "I do not want to be the person you settle for because you have no one else."

Helen couldn't help but notice how ironic his words were, considering who he really was. "Oh, North." She whispered his name softly as she stalled him by putting her hand atop his. "Every day that I am in your presence, I feel like a better person. You are the kindest, most thoughtful, gentlest man I have ever known. You make me laugh, you listen to me, and I can feel you truly care for me, as much as I do you. That is more important than riches or what place you hold in society."

A wide smile stretched across North's handsome face as he peered at her with teasing, narrowed eyes. "You've never told me you care for me. I could see it sometimes when you would look at me, but I like hearing you speak it."

She knew she was blushing, but inside she also felt another pang of shame. The more serious their relationship became, the worse it would hurt when he got his memory back. "Why don't we finish your letter?" she quickly asked, trying to change the subject.

North shook his head at her as if letting her know he knew what she was about. "All right, we'll leave that discussion for another day," he conceded, but she knew he would not be put off for long.

They worked on the letter and finally were able to construct one to North's liking. Thankfully, he didn't seemed to mind, either, when Helen offered to mail the letter herself. She'd hold on to it for a while before writing another one telling Miss Campbell that her brother was missing at sea.

They were just gathering their picnic supplies when a pebble suddenly dropped in Helen's lap, startling them both. "Where did that come from?" Helen exclaimed as she began to look about.

Sam Youngblood stepped out from behind a tree, and he didn't seem happy as he took in the scene before him.

Helen quickly sat back, snatching her hand away from North and receiving a frown from him by doing so.

Excellent. Now both men were unhappy with her.

She was about to ask Sam what he was doing skulking about when he tossed another pebble into her lap.

"Sam, is there a reason for you throwing rocks at Helen? I have to tell you, in our culture, it is not considered polite," North told him, as he stood, then reached down to give Helen a hand up.

Once again Sam eyed their briefly clasped hands with suspicion. "It is my observation that your people consider many things impolite," he countered.

North murmured, "So we're back to the 'your people' issue, are we?"

Helen wondered what that meant as she looked back and forth at the two men. At first she thought North was a little angry at Sam's presence, but now both men seemed to be just bantering with one another as if they enjoyed it.

How much time did these two spend together? Helen wondered, perplexed.

"In our Choctaw culture, throwing pebbles at a woman's feet means you are declaring your intention to marry her," Sam explained as he looked over to Helen and smiled.

Helen had to acknowledge that Sam was actually quite a handsome man, with his dark, golden skin and his straight, black hair that fell to his shoulders. He was quite muscular, too, she easily observed since his attire was minimal, at best. All her life she'd been around men who wore several layers including a shirt vest and sometimes two coats. The American Indians certainly liked to keep things simpler . . . and cooler, it would seem.

"And just what is the woman supposed to do? Throw them back if she doesn't want you?" North asked. He seemed more curious than offended by the fact that Sam was still pursuing her. Didn't he care?

Sam shrugged his shoulders to North's question. "If she agrees to engage herself to the man, she looks at him and acknowledges his presence. If not, she simply ignores him and walks away." He pointed at Helen and smiled. "Since she is looking at me, I'll assume we will soon be wed."

Helen gasped, just a little embarrassed at being caught staring. "I didn't know the rules!" she cried defensively as she threw up her arms. "It doesn't count if I'm not aware of such a custom!"

"Why not?" Sam asked.

Helen gasped and for a moment was unable to speak from being so flabbergasted by the whole thing.

It got worse when North started laughing.

"What is so funny?" she demanded, exasperated.

"You have to admit that throwing rocks at a woman as a way to propose marriage is exceedingly amusing."

"No more than some of the silly customs of your people. I've heard you organize a whole party of people and dogs just to hunt down one little fox. And then you don't eat it!" Sam expressed, clearly disgusted by the waste.

North's laughter turned to interest. "Speaking of hunting animals and such . . . You know, I've thought about the alligator you killed, and I was wondering exactly how you went about doing it."

"Well, I —"

"Pardon me, but could we please get back to the subject at hand?" Helen asked loudly, feeling a little left out. Wasn't she usually the center of both their attentions? What was happening here?

Both men looked at her blankly. It was North who replied, "I'm sorry, Helen. What were we talking about?"

She glared at both men. "It doesn't matter. Please continue with your manly talk of hunting and killing. I'll just gather the picnic supplies and be out of your way!" She let out a dramatic sigh as she whirled around and began to stack the soiled plates, not caring that she was close to cracking them from the force she was using.

As she moved on to the silverware, she realized she no longer heard them talking. Helen wanted so desperately to turn and find out what they were doing, but she was determined to ignore them.

She couldn't believe it when she felt another pebble hitting her back. She whirled around to fuss at Sam and demand he stop doing that, when she saw it wasn't the Indian at all but North who was standing there, tossing a pebble back and forth in his hands and smiling at her. Astonished, she couldn't hold back the giggle that bubbled from her throat.

North grinned as he slowly tossed his last pebble at her feet. Helen looked to see if Sam was still around but noticed he had already disappeared, leaving them alone.

Her eyes returned to North's, and she sauntered over to him. "Are you acknowledging my presence?" North asked teasingly, repeating Sam's words.

"Yes, but throw any more rocks at me, and I just may throw some back."

North laughed again as he helped her gather the remaining picnic supplies and then headed back to the plantation.

A few days later, North was told to go to the bedside of John Paul Hughes, a young man who was a member of his church and the son-in-law of Silas Hill of the Hill plantation. He'd been accidentally shot while hunting, and the doctor was unsure whether he would live or die.

For two days, North did nothing but stay by that young man's bedside, read his Bible, and pray. It was a true test of his faith, as the time seemed to stretch endlessly for himself as well as for the young man's family. He prayed he was saying the right things to them and doing all he needed to do in comforting them.

Finally John Paul's fever broke, and he awoke at the end of the second day. Once the doctor told everyone that his wound had no infection and it seemed he would live, North made his way home with Dr. Giles.

On the way there, North broached the subject of memory loss and asked if the doctor knew anything about it, mostly how long it usually lasted. The doctor, however, told him he knew very little but had known one man who never regained his memory after falling off his roof.

It was not the encouraging news North wanted. He chose to believe instead that God would bring his memory back in His time.

Once he arrived home, as he was turning the corner at the church, the first thing he noticed was Helen sitting on his front porch with Josie and Pierre. It was the most welcoming sight in North's recent memory, and probably in his life, that he'd ever witnessed.

Helen waiting for him to come home.

He didn't even think as he began to jog toward his house. He leaped up the steps, taking them two and three at a time, and walked right up to Helen. North pulled her up from the chair and enveloped her in an embrace.

He felt her hesitate, but only for a second. Her arms were quick to circle his waist and begin patting his back in a comforting gesture.

They stood there for a moment as he slowly let all his tension and anxiety drain away and allowed himself to be rejuvenated by her embrace.

It overwhelmed North sometimes to realize how much he actually loved Helen and how he needed her in his life. He wanted to spend the rest of his days making her happy and showing her how much he loved and adored her.

Josie's giggle, then Pierre's discreet cough, brought him back to the reality that there were other people around them. He, too, began to become conscious of just how inappropriate his actions were.

He backed away from Helen, giving her and the others a sheepish half grin. "Uh,

I'm sorry, but I feel I'm not myself this afternoon. I've not had any sleep since Wednesday."

They may not have totally believed his excuse, but they were willing to give him the benefit of the doubt. Helen quickly took his arm and directed him into the house. "You poor dear! Come and sit down, and Pierre will get you a bowl of soup."

"Yes, of course!" Pierre responded quickly, going to the fireplace, where a huge black pot filled with soup was slowly boiling over a low fire. "You will eat and go right to bed," he instructed North sternly.

North grinned tiredly as he sat down. "You'll get no arguments from me."

Josie slid into the chair beside him and put a comforting hand on his arm. "Shall I go and fluff your pillows and turn back your bed?" she offered, concern clearly written on her small features.

"That would be nice, Josie," he answered, leaning forward to give her a kiss on the forehead.

The younger girl giggled and jumped up to go do the task.

He couldn't help but reach for Helen's hand as she sat by him, looking at him with concern brimming in her eyes. "Have you been here all day?"

She squeezed his hand gently. She began searching his face as if making sure he was all right. "Yes," she answered. "Josie and I wanted to help Pierre clean your house and do some of your chores before you got home. How is John Paul faring?"

"The doctor said he should be fine. But a few times they weren't sure he'd pull through." He stared at her a moment, hoping to convey the feelings he'd felt the last few days. "For the first time, Helen, I finally experienced being comfortable with my occupation. The family needed my strength to lean on and my prayers. I wish I could tell you what peace I felt, as if I were doing something I'd done many times before, performing the deed that God had made me for — ministering to the hurting."

He was about to say more, but Pierre chose that moment to set the bowl of soup in front of him. "We'll talk more about this tomorrow," he whispered before he exchanged a smile with her. He squeezed her hand once more, then let it go to take hold of his spoon.

"Oh, let me get you a slice of bread to eat with that," Helen told him as she got up from her seat to walk over to the counter.

"Just cut a small slice. I'm too tired to eat a lot tonight," he mentioned, then took a bit of the soup, closing his eyes from the warmth and the tantalizing taste of it.

"Yes, Your Grace."

North's eyes widened at Helen's words, and he noticed she, too, seemed frozen, no longer cutting at the bread.

"Your Grace" . . . What did that mean? Why was it familiar, and why in the world did Helen say it?

Perhaps he hadn't heard just right. "I'm sorry, did you say — ?"

Helen whirled around from the counter, and North was perplexed to see panic flashing in her wide eyes. "Yes! Yes, I was about to quote my favorite verse in the Bible!" she said just a little too brightly.

She is quoting a verse? Now?

" 'Your grace is sufficient for me.' " She misquoted, which North noted.

"Uh, I believe it is a part of a scripture that actually reads, 'My grace is sufficient for thee,' " he corrected, still unable to get rid of the feeling there was something important connected with the words and Helen knew it.

"You know, I believe you're right!" she said, her smile just a little off kilter and forced. She placed the bread in front of him on a small dish.

"You know, I just realized how late the

hour has grown!" Helen exclaimed un-
naturally loudly. "We'd better get Pierre to
drive us home and let you get some rest."

"Helen, are you all right?" North asked,
but his question was ignored as she flew to
his bedroom to get Josie.

North rubbed his eyes wearily as the
words *Your Grace* kept ringing in his head,
only it was different voices than Helen's saying them.

"Perhaps you should get into bed, monsieur. I'll be back in a moment to finish
cleaning the kitchen," Pierre told him, and
North wearily agreed as he watched Helen
fly out of his bedroom, towing a reluctant
and confused Josie behind her.

"Maybe I do need some sleep," he murmured, thinking that possibly everything
would make sense in the morning.

CHAPTER 14

Indeed, everything did make sense the next morning when North opened his eyes from a restful sleep. The sun appeared to be shining brightly as beams of light pushed through the openings of his curtains. He listened and thought to himself that even the birds seemed a little more cheerful as they whistled and chirped like never before.

In fact, the whole world seemed to be a much brighter and certainly a much clearer place to live on that particular morning.

And it was all due to the fact that North woke up knowing *exactly* who he was.

And it wasn't Hamish Campbell.

Every last memory North had ever collected and remembered was there for him to pull up at will. Suddenly everything made sense, from his ill-fitting clothes and his being unfamiliar with simple chores, to his feeling at odds with his profession and not being comfortable with public speaking.

The only thing that made no sense at all was why Helen played along with everyone's wrong assumption that he was their long-lost preacher.

Propping his hands behind his head, North thought back to their first encounter in Golden Bay and how shocked she'd been when he hadn't remembered her. Suddenly all the guilty expressions that had flashed on her pretty face and the reluctance she exhibited for telling him any information about his life made complete sense.

The little minx! She actually allowed and even encouraged him to believe he was someone else!

Suddenly he laughed as he realized the length at which she'd gone to keep the truth from him.

Was it done so that she might have a chance with him?

It made him smile even more. Of course she would have thought that way. Helen had no idea he'd spent night after night thinking of some way to convince his family to allow him to marry someone several classes beneath him. He'd never been the sort of person to rebel against his position or want to cause dissension in any way; so when he realized he had feelings for Helen Nichols, a poor farmer's daughter, he didn't know how to tell his mother, friends, or peers.

He'd even tried to tell Nicholas, who had himself married a woman who was a vicar's daughter, but Nicholas had laughed off his feelings, telling him he'd get over his infatuation.

But he hadn't. In fact, North had grown more in love with Helen each time he was with her, and he was sure she felt the same way.

He'd made excuses to postpone his voyage to America and had been glad when the war helped to delay the trip. He just hadn't wanted to be away from Helen that long.

Finally he had found a way to go to America *and* make a way to ask Helen to marry him while being away from his peers and immediate family. After speaking with Claudia Baumgartner, Josie's older sister, about her search for a companion for Josie, he persuaded her to seek out Helen for the position.

He reasoned that once he arrived at the Kent plantation, he would make contact with her and convince her to marry him.

He had a feeling that Helen took the position because she knew *he* was coming to Louisiana.

How sad it was they'd both gone to such great lengths to be together. Especially

Helen, since she had had no idea how he felt about her.

North sat up in his bed as he thought a moment about all Helen had told him. She'd said she had always wanted to better herself. Even Christina, her best friend, had told him that Helen knew everything about the aristocracy and longed to be a part of that world.

He still loved Helen, no matter how much she had tried to deceive him into thinking he was someone else. She had done it because she loved him. That he had no doubts about.

But he wondered if she would love him without all the riches and the titles in front of his name. What if he truly were Hamish Campbell? Could she live the life of a poor minister's wife?

As North slowly got out of bed, he found it hard to concentrate on anything, much less reason out Helen's feelings for him. He found it a bit difficult to merge his old memories with the new ones because he felt like such a different person than he used to be.

In all honesty, he could remain Hamish Campbell for the rest of his life and be completely happy with that choice.

But he had other people to consider

besides himself. He had four large estates that depended on him. If his cousin Wilfred, his next of kin, got hold of them, they would be run to ruins because of his excessive gambling habits.

Then there was his mother, who was the epitome of the proper noblewoman and embraced all of what the ton stood for in style and behavior. But although she could be an extreme snob and terribly bossy, he loved her — even if she did urge him constantly to marry and to marry well.

She would not be happy once he brought Helen home as his wife. But hopefully, after they gave her a grandchild or two, she would forgive him.

As he thought of his family, he tried to imagine what his cousins at the Kent plantation must have been going through. They had probably gotten word he was missing or even dead.

He wondered again if the real Hamish had somehow made it ashore. The man had seemed so calmly resolute in his belief that he would soon die. Perhaps God had prepared him and given him peace. North truly hoped so.

But somebody had to tell his sister! He realized that since Helen had taken the letter they had written to her, it probably would never be mailed. She must have taken it because she had planned to write a new one, telling Hamish's sister that her brother had been lost at sea.

Poor Helen. The more North thought of the situation that Helen had created and how she must have felt when it grew to be more and more complicated, he really felt sorry for her. But it also made him feel humbled she'd done it all for him. If she'd only known he had planned to court her anyway and to declare his love to her, she wouldn't have had to go to so much trouble.

He began to dress himself, pulling on his simply made clothes, and he realized he would actually miss dressing in the simple garments. His usual suit consisted of so many layers and had to be buttoned, tied, and ironed just so, or a person might find his name gossiped about all over London for not knowing how to properly dress. He did hope his own trunks, bearing his fine garments, had been taken to the Kent plantation. Once he told everyone who he really was, he'd be expected to dress appropriately.

Pulling on Hamish's brown coat, he walked to the window and pulled back the curtain. As he looked out to the little white church in his view, he had a moment of regret that he would not get to enjoy being the town's pastor for very long. He knew it wasn't his calling, but he felt the work so much more worthwhile than anything he'd done before.

He stayed at the window a little longer as he tried to decide his next course of action. The one thing that kept ringing in his head was that he didn't want everything to come to an end just yet. Once Helen knew his memory had returned, she might start treating him differently, and so would everyone else. They would have to become adjusted to his being a duke again, and that would take all the fun and excitement out of their fresh, new relationship.

One more week or two as Hamish Campbell surely wouldn't hurt anyone, would it? he wondered, already liking the idea. He could find a way to sneak off to the Kent plantation to assure his relatives that he was all right, but other than that, he could enjoy being at Golden Bay awhile longer.

When Helen woke up that same morning, she was a bundle of nerves over what happened with North the night before. He seemed to react to her slip of the tongue so oddly that she feared she had shaken loose some of his memories.

Did he remember he was a duke?

In fact, she had worried so much about it that her head ached. Imogene suggested she sit out under the cypress trees in the swing and let the cool morning air soothe her head.

So far, it hadn't helped. Sitting so close to the bayou, all she could hear were the crickets and frogs making such a loud noise together in a sort of a fast rhythm that it seemed to go along with the pounding of her head. When a woodpecker joined in the chorus, she finally decided a cold cloth in a nice, dark room might be a better choice.

Helen walked back to the house, and when she was almost to the yard, she heard the distinct sound of a carriage coming up the drive. Squinting through the haze of pain, she finally focused on the driver of the barouche.

It was North, she realized in a panic, making the pain in her head worsen.

But as he jumped from the vehicle and ran to where she was, she noticed he was smiling at her and . . . he was holding a bouquet of flowers!

"Helen!" he called as he waved to her. The closer he got, the less her head hurt. It was amazing, really.

Slightly winded but still smiling, North

trotted to a stop before her as he held out the bouquet of wildflowers. "I'm so glad I caught you outside. I didn't really want to disturb anyone else," he explained as he looked at her with love shining in his gaze.

Helen was relieved he seemed not to remember her odd behavior from the night before. Perhaps he was too tired to remember anything! "You're here early," she commented, hoping he'd reveal the reason for his visit.

"Yes," he answered cryptically, without explanation. "Is there somewhere we can go to be alone? I know it is an improper thing to ask, but I just had to see you and talk to you this morning."

Hmm. What does this mean? "We can go out on the bayou in Joseph's pirogue," she suggested. In the last few days, Sam seemed to be watching for her at the pier as he kept trying to "woo" her, as he called it, by serenading her with his flute.

"Is that anything like a rowboat?" North asked warily.

Helen laughed and tucked her arm into his. "If you're asking if you have to use a little bit of muscle to make it go, then the answer is yes!"

Minutes later, they were paddling down the bayou, searching for a nice shaded spot to stop for a while.

"Oh, look! There are several large oaks over there and an old root sticking out of the bank to tie the boat to," Helen told him as she pointed over his shoulder to show him exactly where it was.

North almost upended the boat as he moved about the shaky vessel to grab hold of the root and then wrap the rope around it. He looked at her and joked, "I'd better be careful! Last time I fell out of a boat, I lost my memory. I'd hate to see what would happen if I did it again."

Helen looked over the boat and could only imagine what was beneath the murky water. "You'd probably be eaten," she quipped with a shiver.

North chuckled as he climbed out of the boat and then helped her up the slightly steep embankment.

As they walked to the base of a huge, sprawling oak, Helen knew she couldn't have picked a more perfect place for them to sit and talk. It was peaceful and cool under the shading leaves with only small rays of sunlight able to peek through.

North dragged a log over so they would have an elevated place to sit and lean against the tree.

At first North and Helen didn't speak a

word — they only sat there enjoying just being next to each other.

"I did a lot of thinking last night and this morning," North finally said in a low voice, as if he didn't want to spoil the mood of their special place.

Helen didn't know what to make of that statement. Did he remember something, after all? Her stomach began to twist in knots with worry. "What were you thinking upon?" she asked, even though she wished only to change the subject.

North sat up and turned so he could look at her. "I thought about you and the feelings I have for you."

Helen's stomach eased a little as he looked at her with such love and gentleness shining in his eyes. "You did?" she asked, unable to say anything else. She wished she could remember some of the clever things her favorite heroines would say during such intimate situations as this.

North nodded and reached to take her hand. As he caressed her palm with his thumb, he seemed to be weighing what he wanted to say next. "And I thought about what your feelings were for me." He continued, watching her cautiously. "Do you love me, Helen?"

Helen's breath caught at the straightforward question. She wasn't expecting such directness from him on such a delicate topic. She felt so conflicted as she looked up at his handsome face. Like a fly caught in the web of a spider, she felt like any move she made would only make things worse. Either saying nothing or confessing would accomplish the same thing.

The truth of the matter was that she did indeed love him with all her heart. There was no way she was going to make him believe otherwise.

"I do love you, North."

A look of pure joy spread in the form of a smile across his face as he let go of her hand and placed both hands on either side of her cheeks. "And I love you, my sweet Helen. You have wound yourself so deeply into my heart, I can't imagine my life without you," he expressed wholeheartedly, then bent forward and kissed her.

Tears borne more of sorrow than happiness stung her eyes, and she returned his kiss, finally letting free all the pent-up feelings she'd kept locked away since she'd first met him. After a moment he moved his lips from hers to string tiny kisses across her cheeks and up to her brow. Then, leaning his forehead against hers, he appeared to be slightly winded. "Marry me, Helen," he said suddenly, startling her so much that she nearly fell off the log.

"What?" she gasped as she pulled back from his embrace. "But you only just asked to court me and —"

He shook his head and interrupted her words. "I know what I feel, and nothing is going to change that!"

He had no idea what he was saying, she thought, growing panicky. "You don't know that for sure, North. Perhaps if we just wait —"

North put his hand over her mouth, a loving smile curving his lips. "I said nothing," he stated firmly and resolutely. "God brought you into my life, Helen. He took a situation that could have been disastrous with my memory loss and then sent you to help me get through it. We were made to live together, raise children, grow old with one another."

Helen looked away in order to try to stop herself from crying again. Once he found out it was she and not God orchestrating this whole situation, he would change his mind about wanting to marry her.

This is such an impossible dilemma, she cried silently, as her panic only grew. If only she had someone to talk to. If only Christina wasn't an ocean away to help her know what to do.

"Helen, I'm sorry," he said gently as he brought her face around with his hand. "I've gotten carried away, haven't I? I've had all morning to think about this, and you haven't had time to let it all sink in."

She shook her head, and a tear escaped despite her best efforts at keeping them at bay. "I'm sorry, North; I guess I am a little overwhelmed."

"And of course I haven't thought about you needing to inform your parents, also," he thought aloud, his hand still caressing her cheek.

Helen smiled as she placed her hand over North's hand. She couldn't help but be amazed at his impromptu proposal and his childlike excitement at the prospect of them marrying. Whenever she had daydreamed about North proposing to her, it was a very dignified and proper picture of North bending down on one knee and placing the family betrothal ring on her finger.

This was so much better than her dreams.

It was just too bad she couldn't enjoy it.

"North, I would like nothing better than to marry you tonight. I want you to know that. It's just that I do have so many things to consider and plan for before we take that step," she finally said, hoping it would stall him long enough for her to come up with a way to tell him the truth.

North gave her a quick kiss on the cheek and then grinned happily at her. "Just hearing you want to marry me is enough for now. I can be patient until you're ready to set a date." He chuckled. "At least I'll strive to be."

As he stood and gave her a hand up, Helen prayed he'd not only be patient but understanding once all was revealed and the truth finally made known.

CHAPTER 15

Sunday arrived, and North found himself actually looking forward to delivering his message. He had begun studying when he sat with John Paul and decided then to speak about Paul's conversion and how God had used miraculous means to get his attention. He wanted to make the point that God had a plan for everyone, and when we weren't truly listening to what He wanted to tell us or we were going our own way instead of the way He would have us go, He'd use all sorts of methods to get our attention.

He'd had no idea just how much that applied to his life until the day before. God had wanted North to learn something, and apparently it wasn't going to be discovered living as he had been, surrounded by wealth and having everything done for him at just a snap of his fingers. North was ashamed to admit it, but though he went to church and always strove to live right, he had really never talked to God — never really prayed and studied the Bible.

His life had been too busy with social events, his estates, and friends. He had even been caught up in the dilemma of what to do about his feelings for Helen. Instead, he should have prayed and asked for guidance about it. God would have led him to the same conclusion that he'd come to himself: They were simply meant for each other. It didn't matter if they stripped him of his title and he had to live out his days as a poor man. His love for Helen was so much more important.

But of course they couldn't strip him of his title. He was already the Duke of Northingshire, and the worst that could happen would be they'd spend a few years being cut by the ton and passed over when invitations for the season were written. He just prayed Helen could bear up to the snobbery she would face once they returned to England.

England, he thought with a sigh and was surprised to realize he felt reluctant to return. He truly liked Louisiana, even though he stayed sweaty all the time and was constantly battling mosquitoes. The people were truly nice and were more apt to cross social borders than those in his homeland. The only thing that bothered him was slavery. Pierre had made him aware of so many atrocities that most white people just turned their heads to, pretending it was a normal part of life.

Today North dressed in his usual black suit, the nicest one that had been in Hamish's trunk. After running a comb through his thick locks (and making a mental note that he really needed to get a trim), he made his way to the church.

Because the weather was so pleasant and unusually cool for late May, there were more people gathered outside the building. Several people walked up to greet him when he was noticed, including a couple of young ladies who never failed to make their presence known to him. He could now remember other young ladies flirting with him back in England, but he was never sure if it was he or the title they sought. So it was a little flattering that these ladies hoped to catch his attention, even though they knew him to be practically penniless.

Helen obviously was not flattered or amused by the women's attention. He noticed quite a determined glint in her eye as she marched over to him and placed herself directly in front of his admirers.

"Good morning, North," she said informally, knowing it would cause speculation from the onlookers, with such a familiar address.

North managed to stifle his chuckle over her territorial behavior but did smile broadly at her. "Hello, Helen," he returned the greeting, playing along with her plan. "I trust you are doing well this morning?"

He was rewarded with a radiant smile. "Indeed," Helen answered, probably not even aware she was looking at him with all her feelings showing clearly on her face.

Of course the same could probably be said of him, too. Their declaration of love was so new and fresh to North that it was hard not to think about it when he looked at her.

"Shall we go inside?" he said quickly before he might find himself doing something stupid like reaching for her hand or kissing her cheek just to be nearer to her.

"I think we might hear wedding bells soon," someone whispered, and he heard a few others agree. Then he thought he might have heard a cry of protest from some of the young ladies walking behind him but thought again that perhaps it was just a bird.

A few moments later, much to the congregation's obvious relief, Miss Ollie sang the last stanza of her hymn and sat down in her pew in the front row. North walked up to the pulpit after that.

As he scanned the room, looking at the faces of those he considered his friends, he felt a real sadness that he wouldn't be with them much longer. Part of him even wished he could continue the work of a minister. It was true he wasn't the best at delivering a message, but he mostly liked just being a regular person, not revered for a title or riches, but counted and respected as one of a small community.

North began his sermon. Because of his renewed confidence from the return of his memory and the fact that he believed in his message so strongly, he was able to preach like never before. In fact, there was a sort of surprised look on the faces of most of the congregation as they stared and listened intently to what he was saying.

Had I been that bad?

When he had finished with a closing prayer, he glanced over to where Helen sat with Josie and the Baumgartners, and he was pleased to see her face beaming with pride.

"That was wonderful!" she whispered to him afterward, when almost everyone had gone.

"Yes, you're like a real preacher now,"

Josie commented, having heard what Helen had said. She had her bonnet in her hand, holding it by the ties and twirling it around.

"Josie! I do wish you would learn to hold that tongue of yours!" Imogene scolded with exasperation. "And would you put your bonnet back on?"

Josie scowled, still swinging it. "But it's too hot!"

Imogene gave her a narrowed look of warning, which made the little girl quickly plop it back on her head.

"You will dine with us today, will you not?" Imogene queried North. "I would love to discuss some of the points of your sermon I felt were particularly inspiring."

With her comments, as well as most of the congregation's, North felt a little overwhelmed by all of the sincere praise, whereas before it had been halfhearted, at best. "I was hoping for an invitation. There is also something I would like to discuss with Mr. Baumgartner."

"Excellent!" Imogene crowed, clasping her hands together at her chest. "You can ride in the carriage with Josie, and I will ride in the barouche with Robert."

North was able to steal a few moments alone with Helen before Josie joined them. "Helen." He called her name softly as he reached across and held both her hands. "I am going to speak with Mr. Baumgartner today about my intentions toward you and that I've ask you to marry me. I know you have not given me a definitive answer, but I feel we should make him aware of our feelings for one another."

North watched the warring emotions play across her lovely features, and he felt a little guilty himself for not telling her he knew the truth.

"But shouldn't we wait until your memory returns?" she fretted.

"What if it never returns? Could you be happy living here with me even though I can barely remember ever knowing you before?"

"Oh, North, I could be happy with you in any place or any circumstance," she declared so passionately that he couldn't help but feel she was sincere.

"And I, you," he responded softly, wishing he was able to kiss her once again.

They heard a sound outside the carriage and quickly sprang apart, sitting back in their seats. Josie stuck her head in the doorway, laughing. "You were holding hands!" she charged merrily as she hopped aboard the vehicle, stumbling over their knees to her seat beside Helen.

Helen lowered her head to shield a blush as she busily straightened her blue dress. "Whatever do you mean?" she hedged.

Josie looked back and forth between them. "I mean I was peeking at you through the window and saw you holding hands." She then turned all her attention to North, her head bent in a quizzical stance. "And whatever did you mean about remembering something or other? Did you ever remember that you once knew Helen before, when you were in England?"

North sent an alarmed glance Helen's way as he searched his mind for a feasible answer.

"A lady does not skulk about listening at doors and spying on her elders!" Helen scolded in the meantime, obviously trying to change the subject from what Josie had heard. "And I see you've removed your bonnet once again! Whatever did you do with it?"

Josie blushed this time. "I . . . uh . . . tied it on Boudreau's head," she confessed, speaking of Miss Ollie's mule that pulled her tiny wagon. The old mule was famous for getting loose from his fence and trampling the neighborhood gardens.

Although North was relieved to find the younger girl had completely forgotten their previous conversation, he looked forward to the day when there were no more secrets to conceal.

"What's he saying now?" Imogene whispered as the three females squeezed together in a small closet that connected the library and dining room. The dividing panels were easily removed so they could move forward to peer through the cracks of the closet door. Helen was bent, trying to peek through the keyhole, Josie managed to kneel down below her, trying to get a better view, and Imogene kept pushing against Helen's back, nearly toppling her over as the older woman tried to peer over her shoulder.

The thing they were all agog to witness was the meeting between Mr. Baumgartner and North.

"I don't know. I can barely hear them," Josie complained, as she wiggled around trying to get comfortable and leaned on her mother's foot in the process.

"Oww!" Imogene hissed. "Do take care, Josie!" They all moved around a bit to try to get more comfortable. "How did you know the boards were removable, anyway?"

"I just discovered it one day," Josie answered easily, and Helen could only guess who she was trying to spy on when she made that discovery.

"He just declared he loves Helen and has asked her to marry him," Josie whispered a little louder than she should.

"Shh!" Helen warned. "They will hear you!" She peered again through the crack. "Uh-oh! Mr. Baumgartner is frowning."

"What?" Imogene questioned as she tried to take a look for herself. "What's wrong with him? Has he forgotten what it's like to be young and in love?"

"Oh, wait!" Josie cried, this time in a softer voice. "He just asked him if he is able to afford a wife. They're quite expensive, Father says."

"How dare he say that!" Imogene gasped, and Helen was thinking it might not have been the best idea to invite her employer along.

"Hmm . . . This is interesting. North just told him he has recently found out that he has an inheritance coming to him," Helen told them as she wondered where this news had come from. She'd only read part of the letter Hamish's sister had written. Perhaps he'd learned of it from there.

But why didn't he tell her about it?

"Oh, look. Papa is smiling!"

Helen squinted to see the men shaking hands. "It appears they've reached some sort of an agreement."

"Oh, I wish I could see!" Imogene complained, pushing even more against Helen. To balance herself, she tried to brace her arms on the frame of the door.

"If you truly love her, then you have my blessing, Reverend. I would imagine that, as you are a man of God, you are being guided by Him, so I can do nothing less than to approve of the match, also," Helen heard Mr. Baumgartner say to North.

"Thank you, sir!" North replied, a wide smile on his face. "God has indeed brought us together. In Helen He has given me more than I could ever have hoped for in a mate."

"Oh, that's so romantic!" Josie expressed with a dreamy sigh.

Helen brushed at the tears on her cheeks. "He is so sweet, isn't he?"

"That is wonderful, and I'm sure Helen appreciates hearing the sentiment, as well."

Helen watched with trepidation as Mr. Baumgartner looked straight at the closet they were hiding in. "Don't you, Helen dear?"

Imogene, still trying to see a little better, chose that moment to lean forward and, in the process, caused Helen to lose her grip on the door frame and fall directly into the door.

All three of them tumbled out of the closet and landed in an embarrassing heap at the men's feet.

Since she was on top of the pile, Imogene was the first to pull herself to her feet. "Well, I must say this is very embarrassing!" she murmured as she smoothed back the curls that had come loose from her hairpins.

Helen and Josie managed to scramble to their feet, both ignoring the men's offer to help them up. "We were just . . . uh . . . ," Josie began, trying to excuse her behavior, as usual.

"Eavesdropping, dear. I believe that's what they call it," her father supplied for her in a droll voice.

"Why don't I call for a pot of tea?" Imogene mentioned brightly, obviously hoping to defuse the awkwardness of the situation. "Better yet — I'll go make some myself!" She began to walk quickly from the room, and Josie hurriedly followed her.

"I'll go, too!"

Helen watched helplessly as they left her to face them all alone.

"You know, I really should take my leave," North said as he looked at Helen. "Would you like to walk me out to the stables?"

Helen looked over at her employer, who smiled at her and nodded. "Have a good night, Reverend," he directed toward North.

"I am so embarrassed," Helen groaned, as soon as they walked outdoors. "It *seemed* like a good idea when Josie mentioned the closet."

North laughed. "Well, at least you know we have Mr. Baumgartner's approval. We only need to try to send a letter to inform your parents now."

"Speaking of letters," Helen began as she was reminded about something he'd told Mr. Baumgartner. "You mentioned an inheritance in the meeting."

"Yes, so you don't have to worry about my being able to support you," he said confidently.

He didn't, however, explain *how* he knew it. "Oh, I know you will, but . . . umm . . . did your . . . uh . . . sister write in her letter about it?" she persisted.

"No, I actually remembered something about it."

Helen's heart started beating faster. "Oh? You've had more memories?"

He looked down at her, the full moon reflecting a soft glow on his face. "A few," he said, as if it were nothing of great concern.

She tried to read his expression to get some idea of what he knew exactly, but it was just too dark to tell. "Well, that's good," she commented lamely, unable to think of anything else to say.

"Oh, I also wanted to tell you that I may be going to the Kent plantation soon."

His words caused Helen to stumble, so horrified was she by what he'd just said. "Why?" she asked, her voice noticeably shaky.

"I heard they are the relatives of the other fellow who was thrown from the ship. I thought I would go there to convey my sympathies and offer them any comfort I can."

This is bad. Terribly, terribly bad.

She turned her head away from him to take a few breaths, trying to calm herself. "When will you go?"

"Tomorrow."

All Helen could think of was running away and finding a good place to cry her eyes out. It wouldn't solve anything, but it might help her feel a little better. Then she thought of another solution that could very well help. She needed to pray! Only God could help her find a solution to the dilemma she'd caused for herself and North — not to mention the entire area of Golden Bay.

Complaining of a sudden headache, Helen left him standing at the stable door. When she reached the porch, she realized that she hadn't even told him good-bye.

CHAPTER 16

Helen spent a restless night tossing and turning as she grappled with what she should do. She had tried to pray, but the guilt she felt was so great.

How could God forgive her when she would never be able to forgive herself?

The more Helen weighed her options, the more she realized there was only one course of action she could take. It was the cowardly solution, but she just couldn't witness the hurt and betrayal in North's eyes when he realized what she had done.

Darkness still filled the early morning as Helen quietly pulled a small bag from under her bed and stuffed as many of her clothes and belongings as she could manage into it. Then, opening the drawer to her night table, she untied a handkerchief that contained all the money she'd earned since coming to Golden Bay. It wasn't a large sum, by any means, but she prayed it would be enough to purchase a passage back to England.

Helen then tiptoed into Josie's room and gently shook the girl awake.

"What . . . ?" she mumbled sleepily, as she tried to open her eyes and adjust to the lamp that Helen had lit beside her bed.

"Shh!" she sounded as she put her fingers over Josie's mouth. "It's me. I need to talk to you."

Josie sat up, rubbing her eyes. She seemed so young in her ruffled sleeping cap and high-necked cotton gown. "What's wrong?" she asked with a yawn.

Helen patted her on the shoulder and regretted she might not see her little friend again. "I have to leave, and I need you to explain to your parents for me."

Quickly she told her the truth of what she'd done and about North not knowing that he was really Trevor Kent. "Everyone will hate me once they find out, so I have to leave," she explained.

"Please don't leave, Helen. Everyone will understand. I won't even complain about my lessons anymore if you'll please stay!" Josie pleaded, tightly grabbing hold of Helen's hand.

Helen shook her head as tears filled her eyes. "I just can't, Josie. I'm so sorry, but I can't," she sobbed as she got up and pulled her hand away.

Josie began to cry, too. "Will you come back?"

"I hope so," Helen whispered as she quickly bent down and pressed a kiss to the little girl's cheek. "Good-bye."

"But Helen . . . !" Helen heard her call out as she ran out of the room and closed the door behind her.

Helen managed to get out of the house without being noticed, but once she'd run a few steps, she realized she had no idea where to go.

Then she thought of the only person who would help her.

Sam!

Although she'd never been there, Helen knew Sam lived down the bayou, so she quickly began to make the trek down to the pier, hoping that she'd be far enough from the house before it became too light.

It was already getting easier to see, as the dark sky began to show streaks of dark pink and orange on the horizon. Helen scurried as fast as she could along the embankment. As she went deeper into the area where the cyprus trees were thick along the border of the property, she could only pray that she wouldn't meet up with an alligator or even a water moccasin. Frankly there were just too many creepy-crawly things to worry about, so if they were around her, she tried not to notice them.

Her running slowed to a breathless stride as the minutes seem to drag by and her bag grew heavier with each step. She felt as though she was now a ways from the house, but there was no sign of any dwelling or camp where Sam might live.

She honestly didn't know what kind of place the Indian would live in. Would it be like the teepees she'd read about? Sam seemed so primitive at times, yet he spoke very well, and Helen always had the impression he was probably more educated and informed on the customs of the white race than he let on.

As the sky began to brighten her path, Helen grew so weary that she plopped down tiredly on a log to rest a bit. Three times she slapped at the same mosquito as she considered she should have come up with a better plan than just running away. If only North hadn't decided to go to his cousins' plantation, then she might have done better, but as it was, there was simply no time to think much less plan.

"Does this mean you've changed your mind?" a voice spoke behind her, startling Helen so much she screamed.

Whirling around, she saw Sam standing there, laughing at her reaction, and that made her mad. "It's impolite to sneak up on someone like that! You nearly scared me to death!" she charged as she placed a hand on her chest as if to steady her racing heart.

Sam raised a black brow as he pretended to check her over. "You look alive enough to me," he teased. With his calm expression, it was quite hard to tell. "So does this mean you want to marry me?" he tried again, this time his expression changing to a hopeful smile.

Helen sighed. "Sam, you know I can't marry you. I don't love you, and I'll bet you don't love me, either."

Sam looked at her as if she were crazy. "A man doesn't choose a wife because of some silly emotion like love! If she's a good woman, hard worker, and likes children as you do, that's all I need." He shrugged. "It's hard to find a good wife with those qualities, you know."

Helen shook her head, needing to get to the point of why she had come looking for him. "Sam, enough about that. I came because I need your help."

He immediately became concerned. "What has happened? Are the Baumgartners all right? That preacher hasn't done anything to hurt you, has he?"

"No!" she quickly assured him. "It's me, Sam. I've done something very bad, and I need your help to get away from here before everyone finds out."

Sam clearly did not believe her. "Helen Nichols, what could you have possibly done that was so bad? You're a good woman."

She quickly blurted out her story, giving him the basic facts and not painting herself as anything but a deceiver and liar. "So you see, Sam, once North arrives at the Kent plantation, he'll know the truth, and then he'll hate me for what I've done not only to him but also the church! The people will be crushed to find out he's not really their preacher."

Sam threw up his hands. "So marry me, and it won't matter if they are upset with you. In time they will forget, and we can have a happy life together."

Helen covered her ears in frustration. "Sam, will you please stop with the proposals! I cannot marry you, for I love North!"

Sam shook his head as if he didn't understand her words. "But since he won't marry you after this, why not me? I may be your only chance to marry once everyone finds out."

She glowered at him. "You're not making

me feel better, Sam. Will you help me get back home or not? I'm not even sure I have enough money to get home."

Sam let out a resigning sigh. "I'll help you, Helen Nichols. My cousin is captain of a merchant ship that makes regular trips to France. He doesn't sail, however, until tomorrow. You might as well come home and stay with us until then."

Helen looked at him, confused. "Us?"

"My elder sister, Leah, has a house next to mine. You can stay with her."

"You have a sister?" she asked, a little too surprised, for Sam scowled at her.

"Yes, and I have a mother, father, and two brothers. Did you think I was raised by wolves?"

Helen thankfully didn't have to answer that question, because Sam bent down and grabbed her bag. "Follow me," he said gruffly.

By the time they reached Sam's and Leah's houses, she'd apologized for everything from turning Sam down to thinking he was so barbaric. He finally accepted her apology, but she could tell he was still miffed that he had been unable to talk her into marrying him.

The cleared area where the two very English-looking cottages were set was surprisingly beautiful and unlike any of the homes she'd seen in the area. They were placed side by side and faced the bayou. There was even a path that led down to a large pier and a swing hanging from a large, shady oak. The houses were painted yellow and blue with white trim and shutters. Rosebushes surrounded both residences, along with various other flowers that Helen knew must be tended to every day, for they were so perfectly groomed.

"What a lovely place you have," Helen complimented as he walked her to the yellow cottage. Before knocking at the door, Sam threw her a glance that said all this could have been hers, too.

A tall, very beautiful woman with golden skin and long, black, shiny hair answered the door. She might have looked like any number of Indians in the area except for her startling blue eyes. "Hello," she said hesitantly as she looked from her brother to Helen with a quizzical expression.

"Leah, this is Helen, the woman I've been telling you about," Sam told her in his straightforward way.

Helen, so fascinated by the woman's eyes and the fact she was wearing a pretty morning dress instead of leather, blurted out, "You are not completely Indian!" As soon as the words left her mouth, she started to apologize, but Sam interrupted her.

"I never told you, but my father is an Englishman. He and my mother live in Brighton, England. So you see, I'm not a complete barbarian," he told her wryly.

Helen was trying to digest that startling piece of news when Leah said with excitement, "You are to marry my brother then?"

"No!" Helen said a little forcibly. When she saw Leah's smile turn to a confused frown, she quickly added, "I mean, I've come to ask Sam to help me get back to England," she told her briefly.

"Why don't you brew us some tea, Leah? We will fill you in on the predicament Helen Nichols has made for herself."

Sam certainly has a way with words, Helen thought morosely, as she stepped into the charming cottage and began to tell her story once again.

When North rode from the reunion with his cousins the next morning, he couldn't help humming a happy tune as his borrowed barouche rolled steadily back toward the Golden Bay plantation and back to Helen. The Kents had been so relieved to see he was alive and had tried hard to get him to stay a few more days with them, but he told them that he must get back to settle his affairs and to make the truth known of who he really was.

He was ready to tell Helen that he knew the truth. They'd played games with one another long enough, and he so wanted everything to finally be in the open with no more secrets between them.

When he finally pulled into the front of the plantation, however, North knew right away that something was wrong. Several neighbors were gathered on horses around Mr. Baumgartner, and he seemed to be instructing them to do something for him.

He looked to the front porch and noticed Mrs. Baumgartner hugging Josie, and both seemed to be very worried about something.

And where was Helen? Why wasn't she outside with them?

As he climbed down from his vehicle, Josie spotted him and ran down from the porch, with Imogene following closely behind her. "Reverend North!" Josie cried as she ran straight into his arms. She mumbled something about Helen into his coat, but she was talking too fast for him to understand.

As his arms came around her to try to comfort the hysterical little girl, he looked worriedly at Imogene. "Where's Helen? Has something happened to her?"

"She's gone, North," Imogene told him, using the nickname she'd probably heard Helen speak so often. "She told Josie about your memory loss, but she also told her something else that might come as a big shock to you." She paused, seemingly having a hard time getting the words out.

"I know, Imogene. I know I'm not Hamish Campbell," he supplied for her, and he watched her let go a breath of relief.

"Then you know that you're . . . uh . . ."

"Trevor Kent, the Duke of Northingshire. Yes, I do know that."

"Helen's really sorry she lied to you, Reverend. . . ." She was cut off when her mother whispered something in her ear. "I mean . . . Your Grace?" she called him, wrinkling up her nose in question as if it didn't sound right. "Anyway, she was crying and saying you would hate her after you found out, so she's decided to go away," Josie explained in one breath.

North's heart felt as though it had dropped to his toes. "Gone? Where could she have gone?"

Imogene shook her head. "She told Josie she was going to sail back to England. I suppose she's found a way to get to the port. We're about to send some men down to look there for her."

"You don't hate her, do you? She didn't mean for all this to happen. She was just trying to get you to like her," Josie pleaded, grabbing hold of his coat.

North took the time to comfort the young girl by putting his hands over hers. "I don't hate her, Josie. I know she loves me, and I still love her. But I need to go look for her." He looked at Imogene. "Tell your husband to keep looking around the area just in case she's lost in the swamps or forest. I'll ride down and see if she was able to get aboard a vessel."

"Take a horse from the stables," Imogene offered, pointing to where one of their stable boys was standing. "Tell him to saddle one for you."

In a matter of minutes, North was on a horse and riding as fast as he could toward the port. He prayed he could remember the directions that had been given to him as the horse darted along the unfamiliar wooded path.

He could hardly believe his eyes when a man suddenly stepped into the path of his horse. He barely had time to recognize the man as being Sam, when his horse reared up in fear and promptly knocked him on his back.

CHAPTER 17

After he finally got his wits *and* his breath back from the hard fall, North pulled himself from the dirt and glared at the Indian, who just stood there staring at him with narrowed eyes. North had been under the impression they had become friends. They'd gotten along famously during their target practice, which had turned into a competitive yet enjoyable archery match.

"What is wrong with you, man?" North yelled at him as he tried to shake the dirt off his coat and britches. "You could have been trampled!"

"I just wanted to save you the trouble of looking for Helen," Sam answered calmly.

North was surprised when Sam mentioned her. "What do mean? Do you know where she is?"

"She's decided to accept my offer of marriage, and I even get to keep my horses." He spoke again with the same even voice.

He could have been talking about the weather; he seemed so nonchalant. Didn't he know North was insane with worry?

"You're lying! What have you done with her?"

Sam's eyes flared at the implied accusation. "If you're asking if I'm holding her against her will, well, think again. She came to me, white man!"

North didn't know what to believe. Surely he wasn't telling the truth, he thought, starting to doubt. Surely she couldn't decide to marry Sam just because she thought North would be upset with her?

"Listen, Sam. I am out of my mind with worry for her. If you can drum up any compassion within your heart at all, you'll take me to her. I have to see her," he told him, trying a different approach with the Indian.

Sam seemed to take an exceptionally long time to study him, as if looking for the truth. "You're not going to hurt her, are you? She seems to think that you hate her now."

North shook his head, growing irritated by the long wait. "I love her! And when I find her, *I'm* going to be the one who marries her," he stressed. "Now, please, take me to where she is!"

Sam had the audacity to laugh. "You were a lot calmer before you remembered you were a duke," he told him, then turned his head toward the woods and whistled. One of his prized black stallions he'd been trying to trade for Helen came trotting out to him. Sam hopped into the saddle, motioned for North to follow, and took off at a run.

North snapped his reins and rode with the Indian until they arrived at two pretty cottages in a clearing. North didn't wait for Sam to show him which one Helen was in. He jumped off the horse and began to call her name.

He stopped short when a beautiful Indian woman walked out of the yellow cottage, her brilliant blue eyes studying him curiously.

North found himself just standing there for a moment looking at her. She had the face and hair of an Indian and the eyes and dress of an English woman. *Very odd and yet very striking, indeed!*

"You are North? The English duke?" she asked in a soft American accent.

He nodded. "Yes. Can you tell me where I may find Helen?" He got to his point right away.

She didn't answer him at first but leaned her head to the side in a thoughtful, contemplative sort of manner. "You won't hurt her, will you? Helen said you would be very upset with her."

North frowned with incredulity. "Why does everyone suppose I am a violent man? I just want to take her back to the plantation."

"I've told him that I'm to marry Helen," Sam said loudly, as he walked to stand by his sister. North saw the twinkle of laughter in his eyes, but he was in no mood to play games with the Indian.

The striking woman merely sighed at Sam's words and told North, "My name is Leah, North . . . or should I call you Lord Kent?" She shook her head. "Anyway, wait right here and I'll call for Helen."

North saw her open her door and stick her head in as if to talk to someone. The door opened wider, and Helen reluctantly walked out. Her face was a mask of guilt, and she only glanced once at him before looking back to the ground.

Was it guilt for what she'd done, or had she truly agreed to marry Sam instead of him? He didn't wait to find out! He stormed right up to Helen and grabbed her by the shoulders. Her eyes flashed at him with surprise.

"Tell me that you are not marrying Sam,"

he demanded, not caring that he might sound like a lunatic.

Confusion creased Helen's brow as she shook her head. "Is this why you are here? You are upset because you believe that I am marrying someone else? Aren't you even upset that I lied to you and made you think you were Hamish Campbell?"

North moved his hands down her arms to link his fingers with hers. "I already knew that, Helen." He brushed her concerns aside, not noticing Helen's fiery reaction to that statement. "Are you or are you not marrying Sam?" he asked again.

It shocked him when Helen let out a cry of outrage and shook off his hands. "You knew!" she cried. "How long did you know?"

North realized his mistake right away. "Uh . . . I got my memory back the morning after you called me *Your Grace,*" he explained carefully.

Helen just stared at him a moment, hurt and anger swimming in her eyes. "And you knew I would be feeling horrible with guilt over it, and yet you said nothing!" He tried to touch her arm once again, but she promptly slapped it away.

"Wait just a minute," North countered, getting a little irritated himself. "*You* are the one who lied to *me,* remember? I was just trying to figure out your motives for deceiving me. *That's* why I said nothing."

"My motives!" she echoed, pointing at herself. "I've been in love with you for two years! I thought you wouldn't consider me for a wife because I'm not of your class, so I simply just made you think you were of *mine!*"

"Are you understanding any of this?" North heard Sam ask aloud to his sister, but Leah told him to shush and kept her eyes glued to them.

Wonderful. In all his born days, he'd never even come close to making a public spectacle of himself.

Until today.

Then North was suddenly struck by something that Helen had told him before. "I am the nobleman you were in love with, aren't I?"

Helen pursed her lips as if she were loath to admit it. "Yes, but as I said, you did not feel the same for me."

"Helen," North said softly as he tried again to touch her arm. He was encouraged that this time she allowed it. "I have been in love with you from the very moment I saw you at Kenswick Hall."

Her eyes widened with surprise and a little

unbelief. "But why — ?"

North caressed her shoulders as he shook his head shamefully. "I didn't know what to do about you, Helen. I've always done what my family expected me to do. So when I knew I wanted you for my wife, I tried to find a way to make that happen in a place where our every move wouldn't be scrutinized or judged too harshly."

"I don't understand," she began to say, and then her eyes widened with comprehension. "You knew I was coming to America! But how?"

He quickly explained how he talked to Claudia Baumgartner about offering Helen the job of companion for her sister.

"I planned to court you once I had arrived and marry you here. We would have had time to get to know one another and be stronger as a couple to face the criticism of my family and the ton."

Tears filled Helen's eyes as she looked at him with dismay. "You mean I caused all this for nothing? You were intending to marry me anyway?"

North folded Helen into his arms to comfort her. As he glanced over her shoulder, he saw Leah and Sam still standing there watching and listening to everything. Leah was even crying a little, dabbing her eyes with a lacy white handkerchief.

"I've had the time of my life, Helen," he assured her, pulling his focus back to their conversation. "God used this to get my attention and to make me aware of how much I need Him in my life." He leaned back a little and framed her face with his large hands. "It's made me realize, too, I should have never wavered in acting on my love for you."

"Oh, North!" she sighed.

"Oh, my!" Leah sighed with another sniff.

"Oh, brother!" Sam groaned, putting his hands to either side of his head as if the whole thing were giving him a headache. "This is getting embarrassing."

Leah elbowed him. "You're just jealous that you didn't win her."

"No," Sam insisted. "I'm just irritated that I have to start this whole courting business all over with another woman!" With that, he threw up his arms and stomped off to his cottage.

"I'll go get your bag," Leah told Helen, leaving them alone.

North took advantage of their absence. He pressed a kiss to her lips and felt his heart leap when she threw her arms around his neck and kissed him back.

After a moment, he looked down at her

and smiled. "Does this mean you are not marrying Sam?"

Helen shook her head, smiling dreamily. "No, I think I will marry you."

"Wise decision."

"I think so."

Two Weeks Later

"You look like an angel!" Imogene sighed as she peered over Helen's shoulder into the mirror. They were admiring the beautiful ivory lace gown that Millie had made for Helen, with its pearl-lined neck and stylish empire waist. Millie came up behind her and placed a crown of pink roses and baby's breath on her dark curls and adjusted the lace veil sewn onto it.

"She sho' nuf is, missus. Sho' nuf!" Millie said as she joined the ladies at the mirror.

"I don't see why I have to have all these flowers stuck in my hair," Josie complained from behind them, causing them all to turn and look at her. She was dressed in pink satin with a circlet of roses in her hair, just like Helen. "I'm not the one getting married, so what does it matter?"

Helen reached for the younger girl's hands and couldn't help but notice how lovely and grown-up Josie appeared in her pretty dress. "But you're my maid of honor! And for that, you get the privilege of wearing roses like me."

Josie let go of her hands and rolled her eyes, letting Helen know the "privilege" wasn't appreciated.

Imogene stepped up to adjust the string of pearls that she'd lent Helen for her special day. "We are going to miss you once you've gone back to England," she said as her eyes grew misty, just as they always did when the subject of Helen's leaving was broached. "It will be quite dull in this big house without you around to cheer us up."

"Yeah," Josie seconded, as she sat down on the window seat. "I won't miss the lessons, but I truly will miss having you to talk to."

Helen blinked back the tears as she rushed to comfort her young friend. "We are to stay for three more months, Josie. We have lots of time to finish your lessons," she teased to brighten everyone's mood.

Josie pretended to be put out by that news, but Helen could see that she was in better spirits.

"We must hurry if we're to get to the church on time!" Imogene said as she looked at the clock on Helen's mantel. "We can't keep Lord Kent waiting!"

Lord Kent. It seemed so strange to Helen

to think of North as a duke anymore. Because he'd offered to stay on for three months as the church council searched for another minister, he still seemed like an ordinary person to her.

But he wasn't. And soon, when Helen became his wife, she wouldn't be, either.

Lady Helen Kent, Duchess of Northingshire. Just thinking of the title made Helen anxious — anxious she would have a hard time adjusting to her new life once they arrived back in England. Could she cope with the censure and the coldness she would receive at marrying so far above her station? She prayed every night that God would help her to do so.

That was one of the reasons she and North decided to marry in Louisiana. Their day would not be ruined by gossip and speculation but could be shared with the people they had grown to love in Golden Bay. Helen did feel a little remorse that her mother and father would not be able to see her marry, but she'd promised them in a letter she'd write down every detail to share with them after it was over.

Of course, there was one other reason they were not waiting to marry in England — North simply told her he would not wait that long to make her his wife.

North had teased he was afraid that Sam would talk her into marrying him instead, but she knew that he was just as eager as Helen to start their lives together.

"Well, I think we are finished here!" Imogene announced as she looked Helen over once more. "Are you ready to go meet your future husband?" she asked with a happy twinkle in her eyes.

"I've been ready for two years!" Helen stressed as she took Imogene and Josie by the hands and laughingly pulled them toward the door.

"Are you sure you want to go through with this, monsieur?" Pierre asked as he helped North don his dark gray overcoat.

North smiled at him, purposely misunderstanding his question. "Of course I want to marry Helen. I'm practically giddy with anticipation!"

Pierre narrowed his eyes and wagged his finger back and forth. "No, no. You know what I'm talking about," he corrected, his face quite serious. "You should reconsider having me stand up with you as your groomsman. It will cause some to walk away and not stay for the ceremony."

North shook his head. "That is why we are holding the wedding outdoors under the oaks. I want everyone who I consider to be my friends to attend, and that includes Sam, the servants and slaves at Golden Bay, and *you*. If someone is offended, then they can leave without causing a commotion," North stated firmly as he checked his hair in the mirror of his dressing table. The fancy piece of furniture as well as the tall four-poster bed looked out of place in the small room, but North had wanted it to be more comfortable for the three months he and Helen were to live there. Once his cousins realized that they could not talk him into living at the Kent plantation, they had generously lent him all the furniture that he needed for his brief stay.

"I don't believe I have ever seen such a crowd of people, monsieur," Pierre observed as he peered out the window. "And I see that Helen has just arrived with the Baumgartners."

North's heart skipped a beat at the mention of her name. He hadn't seen Helen in three days because of all the preparations for the wedding, and he missed her dreadfully.

He vowed to make certain that after today they would never have to be apart.

After one last inspection, North and Pierre walked out of his house and made the short trek to where everyone had gathered. He greeted the minister who had driven from New Orleans and then faced his friends and family, waiting for his bride.

There was a momentary silence as everyone acknowledged Pierre would be standing up with him, but everyone stayed where they were. He glanced around and saw Sam and Leah standing by his cousins, and standing away from the crowd but close enough to see and hear the ceremony were all the servants and slaves from the Baumgartners' plantation.

A violin began to play a sweet tune just as Helen and Josie stepped between their guests and started walking toward him.

North's eyes met Helen's as she drew closer to him, and he felt his heart swell with love and thankfulness. God had given him so much, and that included his heart's desire — Helen Nichols.

When she'd reached him, he eagerly took her hand and tucked it in his arm. He smiled down at her, not really hearing what the preacher was saying until he got to the part about anyone objecting to the marriage.

When they heard someone clear their throat as if they were about to say something, North whispered a name at the same time as Helen, "Sam!"

Horrified, they glanced back to look at the Indian, only to see him smiling benignly at them with a look of mock innocence. Leah had her face covered and was shaking her head in obvious embarrassment.

North quickly turned around and found the young preacher frowning at him. "May I continue?" he asked, apparently perturbed that North seemed to not be paying attention.

North glimpsed at Helen and found her trying to hold back a giggle. "Yes, please do," he stressed, relieved that Sam had behaved himself.

Except for the fact that North heard someone whisper that, as a duke, he *could* have provided benches or chairs for his guests, the rest of the day went off without a problem.

Five Months Later — London, England
"The Duke and Duchess of Northingshire!" the wiry butler announced to the ballroom at large, causing every person in attendance to stop what they were doing and stare at the couple standing at the top of the stairs.

"Oh dear! They're all looking as if they've received the shock of their lives. Wasn't it posted in the *Times* some while back?"

Helen whispered nervously, gripping her husband's arm as if her life depended on it. Even though they were in the familiar surroundings of Kenswick Hall, she still felt like an outsider.

She looked up to see North smiling as if he had no cares in the world. "Of course they know. It's been the talk of the town, if not the entire country. Smile and pretend you don't notice them."

"That will be a little difficult," she said between a clenched-teeth smile.

Carefully they walked down the stairway, and Helen prayed she wouldn't fall, giving them something more to gossip about! They'd spent a wonderful week in North's Bronwyn Castle in Scotland, and though Helen knew that attending her best friend's ball was important, she would have rather stayed up in the Scottish hills with North.

They had just cleared the last of the steps when Christina, her best friend and the Countess of Kenswick, appeared through the crowd with her husband, Nicholas, in tow.

"Helen!" she cried and threw her arms around Helen. "I am so glad to have you back home!"

"I am glad to see you, as well," Helen told her, as she returned the hug and stepped back to look at Christina with surprise. "You're expecting another . . ." She didn't finish her sentence but looked wide-eyed at Christina's slightly rounded tummy.

"Yes!" she nodded happily.

She turned then to greet Nicholas, while Christina warmly welcomed North. Out of the corner of her eye, Helen noticed most of the people had pretended to lose interest in them, but she could see by their glances over their fans and between their gloved fingers that they had not.

"Oh, don't be bothered by them," Christina said, waving a dismissive hand toward the crowd. "You will only be of interest to them until someone else within the ton does something to shock them even more. Then you'll be yesterday's news and merely tolerated."

"I hope so," Helen answered, only to find out later that it was better than even Christina had hoped. Perhaps they had underestimated the power that the Duke of Northingshire wielded, or perhaps it was another sign that God was looking after them.

As the couples walked about the room greeting other people, Helen was surprised to find most were, if not friendly, at least forbearing of her presence.

The one person who she was excited to

see was Claudia Baumgartner. The pretty American girl was truly excited for her marriage and wanted to know all about how her family was faring in Golden Bay.

Finally North whispered into her ear, asking if she would like to step out to the terrace, and she quickly agreed, so tired was she from the stress of anticipating the evening.

"Are you glad to be back?" North asked her softly, once they had walked outside and found a nice private part of the terrace. He placed himself behind her as she leaned on the railing and linked his arms about her middle, hugging her to himself.

"I am, but I am surprised to find I miss Louisiana, too. I would love to go back one day," she sighed, as she thought of how sad everyone had been on that last Sunday there.

"Of course we'll go back. The Kent plantation is partly mine, too, so I'll want to check its progress every so often." He paused, and Helen could sense he was hesitant to ask her something. "Do you regret we married in Louisiana?"

Helen smiled and glanced up at him. "Not at all. Under the oaks with all our friends around us was perfect."

Helen had never felt such love as she

walked toward North as he waited for her by Pierre, wearing a proud smile. He'd looked so handsome in his dark gray suit and white cravat, and so regal, since it was from his own collection of fine apparel.

While it was true the congregation had been saddened by the fact that North couldn't remain as their pastor, they were thankful that they'd stayed for three months while they located a new pastor.

If only the members of the ton could have seen how North and I lived those months after we were married, Helen thought fondly. They had continued to live in the little house behind the church, milking the cow and taking care of the house alone, except for the occasional help from Pierre.

It had been the perfect honeymoon, living so simply and happily together.

There, of course, had been sad moments along their way. The body of the real Hamish Campbell had been discovered by fishermen, and North had the unhappy duty of writing his sister and telling her the bad news.

All in all, Helen believed North had enjoyed his time away from the sometimes stressful job of being the Duke of Northingshire, yet she had worried he would somehow change when he returned to that position.

But she should have known he wouldn't. Even though they were back in England and living in luxury and style, North remained the same as he had been when he thought he was a simple preacher.

"What are you thinking about?" North asked as a breeze blew by, cooling their faces and ruffling their hair.

"I'm trying to picture how your mother would look if she saw you milking our cow."

North chuckled and then placed a kiss on her ear. "I miss Queen Mary. We were just beginning to get along," he teased. "Now my mother is another story." North's mother had still not come around to accepting Helen for a daughter-in-law. But Helen had faith that one day she would.

In fact, Helen's faith had grown tremendously in all aspects as she and North studied the Bible and prayed together. It united and strengthened them so much that Helen knew God could help them overcome anything.

Even the English ton.

Even North's mother, the dowager Duchess of Northingshire!

Helen turned her head slightly to smile up at North and to possibly steal a kiss, but she became distracted when she saw a woman walk to the other side of the terrace and look up into the sky. As the moon caught the curves of her delicate features, Helen could see sadness in her expression and the slump of her shoulders.

The woman was Claudia Baumgartner.

"Now what are you thinking?" North asked as he often did when she became quiet and introspective. He never wanted to be left out of anything . . . even her mind.

"I'm just thinking about a friend who might need my help." Already her mind was whirling with ideas about what she could do to lift Claudia's spirits and help her feel more comfortable with life in England. She'd just finished reading a novel called *Emma*, about a matchmaker who found love herself. Perhaps that's what she could do for Claudia.

North brushed her lips, bringing her thoughts back to him. "You are a very thoughtful friend," he complimented her, smiling into her eyes.

As North looked at her, all previous thoughts jumped out of her head as she reflected again on just how much she loved him. She turned in his arms and placed her arms around his neck. "Now what are *you* thinking about?" she asked, teasingly.

"You," he whispered huskily, as he slowly lowered his head to prove his answer true.